"What's your primary objection to working with me?" Zac asked.

"We have a past," she said bluntly. "You must remember we seldom agreed on how things should be done."

"I remember. And I remember we made it work anyway." A crooked smile tipped his lips.

"Yes, well." She coughed, searching for composure. "It simply wouldn't work, Zac. I'm sorry."

"You could make it work, Brianna. The past is over. There's nothing between us now, after all these years. What happened when we were kids isn't going to affect me now."

His words stung, though they shouldn't have.

Nothing between us after all these years.

Her fingers automatically rose to touch the chain that held the engagement ring he'd given her one Christmas Eve, hidden beneath the fabric of her blouse.

"Don't say no, Brianna. Next weekend is Homecoming. It could be the kickoff for a new plan. Think about it until tomorrow. That would still leave us a week to plan something."

"I'll think about it."

Books by Lois Richer

Love Inspired

Love Inspired Suspense

LOIS RICHER

began her travels the day she read her first book and realized that fiction provided an extraordinary adventure. Creating that adventure for others became her obsession. With millions of books in print, Lois continues to enjoy creating stories of joy and hope. She and her husband love to travel, which makes it easy to find the perfect setting for her next story. Lois would love to hear from you via www.loisricher.com, loisricher@yahoo.com or on Facebook.

Yuletide Proposal

Lois Richer

Love Inspired

™ LOVE INSPIRED BOOKS

ISBN-13: 978-0-373-87783-6

YULETIDE PROPOSAL

Copyright © 2012 by Lois M. Richer

www.LoveInspiredBooks.com

Printed in U.S.A.

O God, you have declared me perfect in your eyes.
—*Psalms* 4:1a

For Barry, with love and celebration
for 30 amazing years.

Chapter One

"Hello, Brianna."

The past ten years had been kind to her former fiancé.

Though Brianna Benson scrutinized Zac Ender's lean, tanned face, she found no sign of aging to mar his classic good looks. Even more surprising, his espresso eyes still glowed at her with warmth in spite of their past.

"Good to see you," Zac continued, inclining his head to one side, a smile flirting with lips that once, long ago, she'd kissed. He bent slightly to thrust out a hand, which she shook and quickly released.

"Good to see you, too," Brianna replied.

Zac had always bemoaned his height because an incident in his childhood to his knee left him unable to play basketball. To extra tall Brianna, Zac's height was an asset not often found among the boys she'd known in high school.

That was only one of the things she'd once loved about him.

"How are you?" he asked.

"I'd be better if you hadn't called me out of a session with one of my clients," Brianna grumbled. She'd been back home in Hope, New Mexico, for two months. She'd been the psychologist at Whispering Hope Clinic where the high school referred their students for counseling for almost that long. So why had Zac waited until today, at ten past eleven, to renew their acquaintance?

He leaned back on his heels, studying her. "You look great."

"Thanks. You're director of education, huh?" Brianna's nerves skittered at the way he studied her. Why was Zac back in Hope? More important, why was she reacting to him like some teen with a crush? "I didn't realize you'd given up teaching."

"I haven't given up teaching. Just changed my focus to administration." His unblinking stare rattled her. "It's been a long time." He said it as if they'd parted the best of friends when actually she'd run away from him on the morning of their wedding.

She raised one eyebrow. The only defense she could summon to battle the emotions he raised was disdain. "That's why I'm here, Zac? To reminisce?"

"No." His head gave a quick negative shake. "Of course not."

Frustrated that her traitorous pulse was doing double time, that her palms still tingled though she'd released his hand, that yet again she couldn't control something in her messed up world, Brianna sighed.

"So would you please tell me what is so important that I had to leave work on my busiest clinic day to come here?" she asked, except she really didn't need him to tell her because she knew with heart-sinking certainty that it was Cory. It had to be. She'd expected returning to Hope would give her troubled son the fresh start he needed to turn his world around.

"Let's discuss this in private. My office is this way." Zac stood back, waiting for her to precede him.

The warmth stinging Brianna's face had nothing to do

with the late-September heat outside and everything to do with the curious eyes of the office staff now fixed on her. She walked past Zac toward the office at the rear of the hall. As she passed, her nose twitched at the familiar pine scent of his aftershave. Some things never changed.

"Have a seat." He sat down behind his large, austere desk only after she was seated. That was Zac, manners all the way. His mother's influence. If only her mother had been like that—caring instead of trying to force her daughter to give up her dream for a business she detested.

You can do anything, Brianna. You just have to believe in yourself.

Zac's words echoed from those halcyon days. But there wasn't much else to remind her of the shy, geeky boy who'd tutored her through junior and senior year so she could win a scholarship to college. Even his bottle-bottom glasses were gone, revealing the hard straight lines of his face. This mature Zac was confident and completely at ease.

"I don't want to say this, Brianna," he began, tenting his fingers on his desktop.

Her fingers tightened on the arm of her chair.

"Your son, er, Cory." He paused.

"Zac, I know who my son is." She steeled herself. "Get on with it, please." Her heart cried at the thought of Cory messing up this last opportunity.

"He was on drugs in school today."

"What?" Brianna gaped at him in disbelief. This was the very last thing she'd expected.

"Yes. In fact, Cory was so wound up, he hit another student in the hallway. Or tried to. Fortunately he missed and passed out on the floor." Zac's voice dropped forcing her to lean forward to hear. "I was really hoping drugs would not be one of the issues here."

What had she brought her son home to?

"Cory doesn't do drugs."

"He took something today." A touch of irritation dimmed Zac's dark brown eyes.

"Is he all right?" She breathed a little easier at his nod and began summoning the courage to go to battle for her son—again—when Zac continued.

"He's a little groggy, but the school nurse assures me the drug has almost completely worn off."

"Cory doesn't use drugs. I mean it, Zac." Brianna held up a hand when he would have spoken. "You've seen his record. He's made a lot of mistakes, but drugs are not one of them."

"Yes, Cory said that, too." Zac leaned back, face inscrutable.

"He did?" She narrowed her gaze. "When?"

"When I talked to him a little while ago."

"Without me present?" she asked sharply.

"I was acting as guardian for the child, Brianna," Zac defended, "Not as an enforcer, or policeman—to give him a penalty. I need to get to the bottom of this, and Cory provided some perspective." He paused. "What I'm going to tell you now is off the record."

"Okay." Brianna nodded, confused.

"I believe Cory was tricked into taking something. He said someone gave him a drink. I discussed his symptoms with a doctor friend who works with emergency-room overdoses in Santa Fe. He suggested Cory may have been given a powerful psychotic." The name of the drug made her gasp.

"That's a prescribed substance!"

He nodded. "The police tell me they haven't seen it in town before."

In spite of the word *police,* something about Zac's attitude reassured her, though Brianna wasn't sure why. "What happens now?"

Zac was silent for several moments. His steady brown gaze never left her face.

"Are you suspending Cory?" she demanded.

"Not at the moment."

"Then—" She arched her eyebrow, awaiting an explanation.

"I've been through this before, Brianna."

"Through what?" She'd expected anger from Zac. Loathing. Disgust. Something different than this—understanding. "You mean you've seen drugs in school before?"

"Yes." Zac nodded. His jaw visibly tensed. The words emerged in short clipped sentences. "Several years ago I taught a student who was also given drugs without his knowledge."

"Oh." She waited.

"Jeffrey had a lot of difficulties at home and at school. The high he got from that one time made him feel he'd escaped his problems, I guess." Zac shook his head, his voice tight with emotion. "It wasn't long before he became addicted."

"I'm sorry," she said to break the silence. Zac clearly struggled to tell her his story.

"Jeffrey called me the night before he died." Zac licked his lips. Beads of moisture popped out on his forehead. "I think he was looking for a reason to live, but I couldn't talk him out of committing suicide." His ragged voice showed the pain of that failure lingered.

"How sad." She ached for the anguish reflected in Zac's dark gaze. He'd always been determined to help students achieve. This tragedy would have decimated him.

"Jeffrey was the brightest kid in the school." Zac's mouth tightened. "He'd already been accepted at Yale. He had his life before him, but because someone slipped him that drug, his potential was wasted."

Brianna didn't know what to say so she remained quiet, silently sharing the grief that filled his eyes and dimmed their sparkle. Suddenly the earlier awkwardness she'd felt didn't matter.

"It's okay." She offered the soothing response she often used at the clinic.

"It's not." Zac's shoulders straightened. His chin lifted and thrust forward. "It's not okay at all. That's why I have to nip this in the bud now."

"Nip this—I don't know what you mean." Dread held her prisoner. Something was going on behind that dark gaze. Would her son be expelled? Would Zac punish her son because of what she'd done?

"I refuse to allow drugs to ruin another young life. Not Cory's. Not anyone's." Zac blinked. His eyes pinned hers. "I'm going to need your help, Brianna."

"My help?" She gaped at him. "I'll certainly talk to Cory, get the whole story and help him understand how easily drugs can cause damage we never expect. But what else can I do?"

"More. A lot more, I hope." Zac rose and began pacing behind his desk, his long legs eating up the distance in two strides. Nervous energy. He'd always been like that. "Let me explain. I came here—actually I specifically chose Hope because school test scores are rock-bottom, the lowest in the state."

She listened attentively as he haltingly told her of the purpose he'd set for himself since Jeffrey had died. Zac spoke of making a difference, of helping kids find their own potential so that drugs weren't even a consideration. His words reminded Brianna of his youthful eagerness to teach when they'd both been students at college, when their goals had been the same—to help kids uncover their potential.

"You must have seen the test scores in the files of the students you've counseled at the clinic," he said.

"Yes." Brianna nodded. "Pathetic."

"Last year was my first year in this job and it was an eye-opener. I found a major lack of initiative, total boredom and a host of other issues. But I never found drugs."

Brianna grew engrossed in his story of trying to create change until she glanced at her watch and realized she didn't have much time to see Cory before her next appointment.

"I'm sorry it's been so difficult, Zac," she interrupted, rising. "Though I don't know the first thing about combating drugs in schools. Education is your field." His slow smile and those bittersweet-chocolate eyes, glittering with suppressed excitement, made her pause. "What?"

"You know a lot about motivating people, Brianna. You always did, even before you started practicing psychology. Inspiring people is in your blood." He held her gaze with his own. "I doubt that's changed."

Surprised that he'd harked back to a past that could only hold painful memories for both of them, Brianna frowned.

"Remember when there were no funds for our school choir to go to that competition?" Zac's grin flashed. "You were the one who roused everybody and got them to pitch in and raise money for the trip."

"You want me to raise money?" she asked dubiously, confused by his excitement.

"No," he said and continued as if she hadn't interrupted. "When Jaclyn's sister died, you were the one who made a schedule to ensure her friends would be with her during the first hard days after the funeral. You were the one who helped Jaclyn solidify her goal for Whispering Hope Clinic, and you were the one who kept that dream alive even though your other partner left town."

"It wasn't just Jaclyn's goal. Jessica was my dearest

friend. I vowed to keep her memory alive by making sure no other kid ever went through what she suffered because of a lack of medical help. That's why I came back to Hope, to help kids," she said.

"I know." Zac smiled. "You're an encourager, Brianna."

What was with the trip down memory lane? It sounded as if Zac was praising her, but that couldn't be. Brianna had jilted him!

"You're a motivator who inspires, and you're very, very good at it. I've always admired that about you."

Admired her? Brianna bristled, irritated that his memory was so selective. The words spurted out without conscious thought.

"If you admired me so much, how come you betrayed me the night before our wedding?"

That was so not the thing she wanted to say to Zac Ender after ten long years. Brianna clapped a hand over her mouth and wished she'd never answered his summons this morning.

"I—wh-what?" Zac's face was blank, his stern jaw slack.

Brianna had to escape.

"Look, I have to go. I have another appointment." She grabbed her purse and headed for the door. "Perhaps we can talk about this again another time," she murmured.

"Count on it."

The firm resolve behind his words startled her into turning to look at him.

"We're not finished, Brianna."

She wasn't sure whether that was a threat or a promise and she didn't want to consider either at the moment. For some reason she couldn't figure out, Zac still got to her. She needed time to get her defenses back up.

"I'll talk to Cory," she promised and left.

Brianna breathed deeply as she headed back to the clinic.

Once there she paused a moment to study the exterior of the building that housed Whispering Hope Clinic and to remember how the dream had started. Jessica's cancer had been diagnosed too late because of a doctor shortage in Hope. As they watched the disease decimate her, Jessica's sister, Jaclyn, Brianna and their friend Shay had made a pact to one day return to this little town in New Mexico and open a medical clinic for kids to ensure no child ever went without help again. Jaclyn was now the pediatric physician at Whispering Hope Clinic. Brianna was a child psychologist and hopefully Shay would soon join them to offer physiotherapy.

Brianna's mother had never understood how deeply Jessica's death had affected her daughter, or how that death had prompted Brianna to volunteer in the hospital's children's ward. But it was there Brianna had learned to listen. That's what she'd been doing on the school steps one afternoon with Shay and Jaclyn. A teacher had later commented on her ability to encourage, and then urged Brianna to consider becoming a counselor. Desperate to escape her mother's expectation that she take over the family business, Brianna focused on her own plan—attend college, get her doctorate and return to Hope to keep her vow. Her mother's refusal to help her reach that goal sent Brianna to seek help from the smartest kid in school, Zac. Once she'd thought he loved her but his perfidy had sent her away from Hope and she'd struggled to achieve her goal on her own.

Now that she was finally back in Hope, fulfilling the dream she'd cherished for so long, Brianna could not afford to get sidetracked by handsome Zac Ender.

Zac ran every evening after sunset, when the community of Hope was nestled inside their houses with their families around them. Usually he used the lonely time to review his progress in reaching his goals. But tonight his thoughts wandered back ten years to a time when he'd been so certain life couldn't get any better; when Brianna Benson said she loved him and he'd loved her.

Zac knew now that he'd been deceiving himself. What did he know about loving a woman? He hadn't had a father growing up, nobody to teach him anything about relationships, especially how to be the kind of husband Brianna needed. He'd always had a social disadvantage. Those first few years after the car accident that had killed his father had left Zac so badly injured he'd had to endure ten years of surgeries just to walk again. Maybe that's when the lingering feelings of abandonment had taken root; maybe he was a loner because he'd never had a role model to show him how to become a man who could open up to a woman, to expose his deepest fears and his worst scars and trust that she would still care for him in spite of everything. Maybe that lack of inner harmony was why he never felt God had any particular use for a man like Zac Ender.

But for that tiny space in time ten years ago, Zac had believed marriage to pretty Brianna was the answer to his prayers. Then, her long, coffee-colored curls had framed her heart-shaped face. Her perfect white smile had engaged everyone and her hazel eyes had sparkled gold glints in their green depths as she'd cheered him on. Zac had bought into her dream that he could finally shed his inhibitions and open up to people as she did, without freezing up. For a little while he imagined it was possible to shed the inner lack of confidence which had branded him a laughingstock from the first awkward day his health had improved so much he'd finally been granted permission to quit homeschooling. He'd walked into Miss Latimer's seventh-grade math class full of excitement and found he couldn't answer a question he'd studied two years earlier. Instead he'd stuttered and stammered until Miss Latimer had called on someone else. Even now, all these years later, the sting of the other kids' snickers and scorn still caused a mental flinch. As time passed, Zac had accepted their branding of the nerd who never fit in.

But in college, Brianna tantalized him with a self-concept that hinted at the possibility of him becoming poised and able to communicate in any situation. Though Zac had improved his communication skills thanks to Brianna's tutelage, he now recognized that back then, inside, in the recesses of his heart, he'd never outgrown being that ashamed, embarrassed kid who couldn't use words to express what was on his mind. Secretly, even then, he'd always feared that one day the vivacious, energetic and exuberant Brianna would realize he could never be the outgoing husband she wanted, that God simply hadn't made him that way. The day her dad told him Brianna had run away from their wedding, the bubble of Zac's pretend world burst.

Now, ten years later, Brianna had changed, and not just by cutting her hair into a pixie style that framed her face and made her eyes the focal point. Zac had changed, too. He knew who he was and exactly what his failings were. He *was* a nerd and he didn't fit in. God didn't mean for him to be a missionary or a minister. He didn't gift Zac with social abilities. Zac still struggled to speak in public. Certainly God didn't expect him to express his faith publicly, other than by attending church. Zac had no illusions about God ever turning him into a public figure. But Zac had a plan. And he'd done what he planned, gotten his degrees, advanced his career. He'd set very high goals for himself. None of them included romance. He had no intention of failing twice.

But now Zac had reached all his objectives save one. It was time to climb the final rung and prove to the world that nerd or not, Zac Ender wasn't a failure. It was time to make his move from delivering education to formulating curriculum. To do that, he needed success. He'd chosen Hope High School as his proving ground.

Success in the only field he was good at was achievable, particularly if he could get Brianna's help.

Zac thought he'd feel awkward with her today. But after the first few moments he hadn't. It seemed natural to seek the opinion of the school division's psychologist about a matter relating to school issues. He'd kept things cool and businesslike between them. No emotion, no harking back to their past mistake.

Until she'd made that comment "How come you betrayed me the night before our wedding?"

Zac jogged up his driveway and made his way to the back deck. He stretched out, gasping for breath as her words played over and over. Finally, when his breath evened, when he'd settled into a patio chair with a bottle of water and still no explanation for her comment arose, he decided it didn't matter.

Their past was over and so was any relationship he'd had with Brianna. It was the future he had to focus on. He didn't intend to waste a second of it rehashing who had done what. She'd come home to Hope. At the first job opportunity Zac intended to leave.

In the meantime he would seek Brianna's help for the school, he'd work toward straightening out her son, but he would not allow any of his old feelings for her to take root. He couldn't. Because some things never changed.

Ten years had proven nerdy Zac Ender was still not the man Brianna Benson wanted.

Chapter Two

"**I**'m leaving now, RaeAnn—"

Brianna stopped midsentence, surprised to see Zac in her office doorway.

"Hi." He grinned.

"Hello. Uh, I'm just on my way to the nursing home. Mom needs…" She frowned. "Did we have an appointment?"

"No." Zac turned, picked up something and carried it in. "Since you declined my offer of lunch, twice in the past two days, I might add," he reminded, one eyebrow arched, "I figured you must be too busy to go out, so I brought lunch to you." He set the basket on her desk and began unloading it. "Voilà."

Wonderful aromas filled the room, catching Brianna off guard.

"Uh, that's really nice, Zac." She blinked. "But—"

"I'll drop off whatever your mom needs on my way back to the office. Okay?" He stood waiting, looking every bit the professor his friend Kent always called him.

"But—"

"I really need to talk to you, Brianna. Today." Clearly Zac wasn't leaving.

Brianna decided it was best not to argue given that every-one who was still in the waiting room had probably seen or heard his arrival. Hope wasn't a big town. She could imag-ine news of his visit to her office would spread like the flu that currently kept Jaclyn so busy. If the intense scrutiny the townsfolk gave her now was what Zac had to endure after she left, Brianna was amazed he'd ever returned.

Why *was* he back? It couldn't be just the failing stu-dents. According to the television reports, there were fail-ing students all over the country. Why had he chosen to return to Hope?

"Have a seat." Zac pulled forward a small table and snapped a white tablecloth in place.

"Where did you learn to do that?" She stared as he set the table with a flourish.

"I ran out of funds before I finished my PhD so I waited tables." He grinned. "Why do you look so surprised? As I recall, you always told me I had to get out in public more to develop my poor communication skills."

She had, many times. But Brianna did *not* want to hark back to those days and be reminded of the many other things they'd said to each other, especially their promises. So she waited until he'd finished, took the seat he indicated and accepted the plate he offered.

"This is about Cory, isn't it? I did talk to him and he still denies deliberately using drugs."

"I know. We'll get to that," he promised. "For now let's eat."

She took a bite. Chicken salad—her favorite.

"This is really good. I've been to all the food places in town and I never saw this on the menu." Brianna savored the hint of lime. "I haven't had a decent chicken salad since I left Chicago. So where in town did you get it?"

"I made it," Zac answered.

"You?" She stared in disbelief. "But you never cooked." That was a stupid thing to say. In the past ten years, Zac had probably done a lot of things he never used to, just as she had.

"The cook at the restaurant where I worked couldn't read. I taught her. She taught me how to make stuff like this." He shrugged. "You used to eat chicken salad a lot in college. I figured you might still like it."

"I love it." As thoughtful as he'd always been, Brianna mused as she bit into a roll. She frowned, then held it up, looking at him with eyebrows raised. "This, too?"

"Nope. Sorry." He shrugged. "Just not that talented."

"Thank goodness." She made a face. "I was beginning to feel intimidated."

"Hardly." He poured a cup of iced tea from a thermos he'd brought. "Nobody intimidates Brianna Benson."

Brianna stared into Zac's face, unsure of whether he'd meant that as sarcastically as it sounded.

"How is your mother, by the way?" he asked.

"Fine." Brianna let his previous comment go. Zac was always sincere. If he were trying to get a dig at her, he'd do it openly. "She told me you've stopped to see her several times."

"I go to the nursing home a few times a week to visit Miss Latimer. She was so good to Mom before she died that I try to repay the favor." For a moment Zac peered into a distance as if remembering the sweet gentle mother who'd encouraged him through countless surgeries after a car accident that had killed his dad and left five-year-old Zac with multiple injuries. "How is your father?" he asked. "I haven't seen him lately."

"Dad's doing better since his heart attack. He visits Mom a lot." Brianna didn't add that she didn't understand why her father went so faithfully when it seemed all her mother did was carp at him.

"I'm sure he's glad you're back."

"I guess. It seems weird to be living at home again, but Cory does the yardwork and I try to keep the house up. We're managing." She finished her salad and sipped her tea, scrounging for the courage to ask the hard questions. Finally she just blurted it out. "Why are you here, Zac?"

For a moment she thought she saw regret rush over his face. Which was silly. Granted it had been years, but she'd pushed into adulthood with Zac and grown to understand him. He was the type of man who never regretted his decisions. He thought through everything, weighed the pros and cons and made his choices only after he'd done a complete analysis. He didn't have regrets.

So what did he want with her?

"What did you mean when you said I'd betrayed you?" Zac looked straight at her and waited for an answer. A frown line marred the perfection of his smooth forehead.

"It doesn't matter. Let's forget the past and deal with now." Brianna took control of the conversation, desperate to avoid delving into the past again. "You want to find out who is giving out drugs and stop the spread of them in the school. I get that."

"Oh, I want a lot more than that, Brianna." Zac's voice oozed determination. "I want the students in Hope's schools to shake off their apathy and start using the brains God gave them. I want them to begin looking at the future with anticipation and eagerness."

"But—" Brianna closed her lips and concentrated on listening. When Zac became this serious it was better to let him just say it.

"Do you know that less than one percent of the students graduating from Hope High School go on to college?" Zac huffed his disgust. "And no wonder. They have no interests. There's no choir, no debate club, no science club, no language club. Everything's been discontinued. And regular class attendance is a joke. *That's* what I want to change."

Brianna blinked at Zac's fierce tone. "Okay, then."

"And I want you to help me do it."

"Me?" She could say no more because he interrupted again.

"I am not a motivator, Brianna." Determination glittered in his eyes.

"That's not true," she said firmly. Zac had motivated her time after time when he'd tutored her to win a college scholarship and all through the courses that followed. *You can do anything you want,* he'd repeatedly insisted.

"If there were even a spark of interest, I could work with that." He frowned at her. "But throw drugs into the mix and the challenge expands exponentially. I need a big change, something that will grab the students' attention."

Brianna didn't know what to say. Zac sounded so forceful, so determined. Intrigued by this unexpected side of him, she decided to hear him out.

"I know you haven't been here long, but think about the kids you've seen at the clinic." Zac's brown eyes narrowed. "Have you spoken with any who are excited about their future?"

"Uh, no."

"No." Zac's cheeks flushed with the intensity of his words. "The world is theirs for the taking but they don't care. They're completly unengaged. Truthfully, so are most of their teachers. They don't want to be, but you can only live with apathy for so long before it seeps into your attitude." He exhaled and stared straight at her. "What we need is something to ignite interest so kids, including Cory, can get excited. That's the only alternative I know to the pervasiveness of drugs."

Brianna blinked. Wow. The old Zac had not been a man of words. This was the longest speech she'd ever heard him give and his passion was evident.

Of course she knew all about Zac's teaching ability, not just from firsthand experience when he'd patiently tutored her, but she'd seen it while they'd studied for their undergrad degrees. Over and over she'd witnessed the way he'd throw himself into explaining a subject. In those days he'd never accepted her praise or seen his ability to instill interest as unique, but it was his skill as a teacher that had taught her to focus on what she wanted and channel her energy into getting it. He called her a motivator back then, too, but he'd been an encourager for her.

If only Cory could find someone like—

Zac.

In a flash of understanding Brianna realized that Zac was exactly who Cory needed to help him find his way. She'd worked hard to be both mother and father to her son, but she'd failed him somehow. Still, this wasn't the time to stand by and let drugs or anything else ruin his chance to begin again. Brianna needed help.

But Zac?

Brianna had thought she knew what it took to raise a child properly—exactly what she'd always yearned for. Love, and lots of it. But the older her son became, the more Brianna's doubts about her parenting ability grew. Love wasn't breaching the growing distance between them. She was failing her own son.

Still—Zac as Cory's mentor? He wasn't even in the classroom anymore. Brianna spared a moment to wonder why Zac, who had teaching running through his blood, had chosen to move to administration.

"Will you help me, Brianna?" Zac's face loomed inches from hers.

The earnest tone of his voice made her blink out of her memories.

"Uh, help you—do what exactly?" Every sensitive nerve in Brianna's body hummed when he leaned close. In ten years she hadn't given as much thought to their past as she had since seeing Zac the first day in his office. And she didn't like the feelings it brought. "Look, Zac, I don't think—"

Brianna stopped. How did you tell your ex-fiancé you didn't think it was a good idea for you to work with him because he still made you feel things?

Her heart raced, pitter-pattering like any high-school junior's did whenever she saw the local heartthrob. She was nervous, that's all. After all, this man was asking a lot of her, and he'd betrayed her once.

"Listen, Brianna. Last night I learned that Eve Larsen had overdosed on drugs." Zac tented his fingers.

"Jaclyn called me in for a consult." She frowned. "What has that to do with Cory?"

Zac sat back, shifted, and then finally lifted his gaze to meet hers.

"Until Cory's incident I had no idea that Hope—that the school—that *we* had a drug problem."

"Maybe you don't."

"It's the start of one. Hear me out, Brianna." Zac stared at her as if she had something smeared over her face. "I've worked where the schools become infested with drugs. They creep in and then take over if nobody stops it. Once they're in place, it's desperately hard to get rid of a drug problem and loosen their grip on the student population. Believe me, I've tried."

"So?"

"So when Cory's case was thrown at me, I knew I couldn't ignore it, not when I'm responsible for the rest of the students. He's a very smart kid, Brianna, but he needs a challenge, something that tests his current beliefs about the world. He needs to be forced to use that brain." Zac paused, his glance holding hers. "As I understand it, so far Cory's been involved in misdemeanors, petty stuff—minor theft, nasty pranks, breaking his curfew—the kind of things that have repeatedly sent him to juvenile court."

"Yes." She was ashamed to hear Zac say it.

"And before you moved here, his last act was to join a gang. Not exactly the remorse a judge is looking for, which is probably why he gave Cory until Christmas to clean up his act and threatened him with juvenile detention if he doesn't."

"That's what the judge said to me," Brianna admitted.

"So you thought you'd move here, and Cory would turn around." Zac leaned forward, holding her gaze with his intense one. "I'm very afraid that Cory's not going to find the challenge he needs in Hope, Brianna. Not the way the school is now."

Brianna sat back, concern mounting as she absorbed the impact of Zac's words. She understood what he wasn't saying. She'd arrived at Whispering Hope Clinic believing her work here would be much easier than her old job. But in the past few weeks she'd begun to question her ability, to wonder if she'd ever get the response she needed in order to help these kids.

"I know a little about drugs," she murmured. "I did some practicum work with kids who were using. For most of the clients I saw then, the best I could offer was a listening ear."

"Don't you want to do more for Cory, much more?" Zac remained quiet, waiting for her to assimilate what he'd said.

In that silence, Brianna recognized the depth of his concern. His brow was furrowed—fingers clenched, shoulders rigid. The Zac she remembered only worried when something was out of his control.

"Do you think the drug situation in Hope is so bad that Cory's future is out the window?" she asked, nerves taut.

"Not yet." Zac shook his head.

"Then what are you saying?" she asked, holding back her fear.

"I'm saying that without something to counteract the drugs—and soon—there's potential to ruin a lot of lives, including Cory's. I'm asking for your help to create that counteraction."

"How?" she asked cautiously.

"I'm not sure yet. That's the problem." Zac dragged a hand through his short hair, a familiar gesture that showed his frustration with having to go outside himself and his resources to accomplish something. He glared at her, his eyes intent. "When it comes to administration I'm the best you'll find."

"And humble, too," she teased. Zac glared. "Sorry. Go on."

"I can set the rules. I can find f-funding for programs. I can insist the teachers go beyond the usual to meet student needs…" The stutter proved Zac was moving well out of his comfort zone with his plea for help.

"But?" she prodded, confused by his words and his manner. Belligerent but beseeching.

"But I can't get inside their heads." His eyes glittered with suppressed emotion.

Suppressed emotion? Cool analytical Zac?

"I insisted the board hand over student counseling to Whispering Hope Clinic, to you, because the kids need somebody who's engaged in their world, not a visiting counselor who will listen to them for an hour here or there, then disappear. They'll see you on the street, in the café, at the grocery store. And they'll know you are interested in them because that's who you are. You're a genuine nurturer, and they'll recognize that." He exhaled heavily.

"Thank you," Brianna murmured, surprised by his generosity.

"I'm the authority figure. But you—you're outside the school system, new in town, fresh from the big city. They'll accept ideas from you. That won't be a problem."

"A problem for what?" She felt totally confused.

"For getting rid of the apathy that shrouds Hope. You don't carry any baggage about Hope."

"I don't? You're dreaming, Zac." Brianna glared at him, hoping to remind him of their past.

"I meant preconceptions about these kids that would block you from seeing potential in them." Their gazes locked before he looked away. "Knowing you, I'm pretty sure you're brimming with ideas of what you want to accomplish in your practice. Innovation. Change." He nodded. "That's what I want, too."

Brianna now had an inkling of where Zac was going with this and she didn't like it. She did not want to work with him. She did not want to rehash all her old feelings of regret and rejection and get bogged down in them. Mostly she didn't want to go back to those horrible hours and days after their almost-wedding when she'd struggled with the rightness of her decision to leave Hope and Zac.

"Just spell out what you want from me, will you, Zac?"

"Okay, I will." He inhaled. "I need a plan to get these kids motivated. Hope isn't like it was when we grew up here, Brianna." He hunched forward, his face as serious as she'd ever seen it. "These kids aren't gung ho about their future."

"Not all of our peers were when we were growing up, either," she reminded.

"Maybe not, but the vast majority of this generation of Hope's kids have stopped imagining bigger or better. I want you to help me change that."

Brianna stared at him, amazed by the passion in his voice.

"Aren't you going to say anything?" he grumbled.

"I don't know what to say," she admitted. "It's a laudable goal and I wish you success, but beyond that, I don't see what I can do. I've already got a lot on my plate," she reminded. "I've barely started at the clinic."

"You'll be busy there. Because you represent hope." He nodded. "That's exactly what I want to give these kids, including Cory. Hope." His voice dropped, his eyes melted. "Please, Brianna. Help me do that."

She'd said that to him so many times in the past. *Help me, Zac.* And every time Zac had patiently helped solve her issue—whether it was schoolwork or peer issues. He even let her bawl on his shoulder when her mom's controlling threatened to destroy her dreams, though she'd been too embarrassed to tell him the truth about the rift between her and her mother. Yet through all her problems, Zac had always been on her side.

Until the day before their wedding.

Brianna veered away from that, back to the present.

"You have to get back to work and so do I. Let me think about it, Zac." When he would have protested she cut him off. "You've obviously been considering this for a while, but it's all new to me. I don't know that I can take on something else until I've got my world settled a little better."

"What's your primary objection?"

"We have a past," she said bluntly.

"So?" His chin jutted out.

"You must remember we seldom agreed on how things should be done."

"I remember. And I remember we made it work anyway." A crooked smile tipped his lips. His grin made her blush.

"Yes, well." She coughed, searching for composure. "You'd want to be rid of me after our first argument. I can't afford any negativity. This is my career and I've worked really hard for it." She tried to soften her words. "It simply wouldn't work, Zac. I'm sorry."

"You could make it work, Brianna. You always had ten irons in the fire and you never had a problem." His voice dropped to a more intimate level as his gaze searched hers. "The past is over. There's nothing between us now, after all these years. What happened when we were kids isn't going to affect me now. How about you?"

His words stung, though they shouldn't have.

Nothing between us after all these years.

Her fingers automatically lifted to touch the chain that held the engagement ring he'd given her one Christmas Eve, hidden beneath the fabric of her blouse. She recalled the many times she'd been down, on the verge of quitting, and had touched that ring, mentally replaying Zac's voice encouraging her to focus on what she wanted and go for it. He didn't know it, but he'd gotten her through so many hard times.

"Don't say no, Brianna. Next weekend is Homecoming. It could be the kickoff for a new plan. Think about it until tomorrow," he begged. "That would still leave us a week to plan something."

"Why does inspiring these kids mean so much to you?" she asked curiously.

"Because of Jeffrey." His voice was raw.

She frowned, not understanding.

"I failed him." Zac's tightly controlled voice held fathoms of pain. "I don't want any more kids on my conscience."

His anguish wrenched Brianna's heart, but the thought of working with him made her knees knock.

"All I can promise is I'll think about it." Brianna rose.

"Good enough." He rose, too.

"Thank you for lunch. It was very nice." *Nice?* It was the most interesting lunch she'd ever had. And that's what worried her.

"You *can* help, Brianna." Zac touched her arm, and then as her skin burned beneath his fingertips, he let his hand fall away. He gathered and stored his things. "Please consider it seriously."

Brianna nodded, handed over the package for her mother when he insisted and watched him leave. Her caseload at the clinic left little time to think about what Zac had said until later that night when, after another argument about his curfew, Cory finally went to bed. She tried to talk to her dad but surprisingly he encouraged her participation with Zac.

"Let the past go, Brianna. Otherwise it will eat you to death."

If it were only that easy.

When he retired and she was alone, Brianna pulled out all the arguments and pieced them together in her head.

Zac made a good case, but despite his intensity and passion, she had a hunch he hadn't told her all his reasons for wanting this project. And forget what he'd said about their past being over; their past was a minefield of things not said. Resentment stirred like a boiling cauldron inside her. Zac, no doubt, carried his own grudges. Sooner or later he'd want to see her pay for running out on him.

Brianna ached to forget the past, but seeing Zac again revived the sense of betrayal she still felt, made worse since Jaclyn had announced her pregnancy. She and Kent were building their future. What was Brianna's future? Cory would grow up, leave and she'd be alone.

She knew love like what Kent and Jaclyn shared wasn't for her. She'd given that up when she'd left Hope ten years ago. That's why she married Cory's father, because it didn't involve her heart. But she was finally doing the one thing she'd dreamed of all her life—counseling kids. She would not be swayed from that goal.

Like a movie, the night of their rehearsal dinner replayed in her mind.

You're right, Mrs. Benson. We'll stay in Hope for a while. Brianna will work in your interior-design store, maybe even take over for you.

With those few words Zac had derailed her dreams, broken every promise he'd made her and destroyed her faith in his integrity. He hadn't known all the details of her battles with her mom, but he had known that Brianna never wanted to return to the store when she'd left after high school, despite her mother's determination that she do so. And yet, he'd promised her mother Brianna would do the one thing she'd always fought against. He'd betrayed her.

Now he wanted her help.

How could she say yes after he'd destroyed the trust she had in him?

How could she say no when he was trying to help kids—kids like Cory?

Sighing, Brianna pulled out her Bible and read a couple of chapters. But they were just words. God, as usual, seemed far away. Still, ever hopeful, she reached out.

"What do I do, Lord?"

The empty silence left her aching with the familiar feelings of heavenly abandonment. Where was God when she needed Him?

It was going to be another sleepless night.

Chapter Three

There were very few times in his life that Zac regretted his actions. Yesterday's plea to Brianna ranked right up there.

He stabbed the button on his phone that paged his secretary.

"Tammy Lyn, would you get me the number of that counseling outfit in Las Cruces, please?" Zac would find his own solutions. Because somehow, he was going to get that state job.

"I will. And I have Brianna's office on line two. She wants to see you between her appointments tomorrow. Do you have a time preference?"

She was going to refuse. Zac was surprised by the rush of disappointment that swamped him. Had he really been looking forward to working with his former fiancée—the one who'd caused him so much embarrassment?

And why *had* Brianna run away on their wedding day? Zac wasn't sure he believed her mother's explanation that Brianna had realized she was too immature for marriage.

"Zac?" Tammy Lyn's impatient reminder snapped his daydream.

"Sorry." He swallowed, firmed his voice. "Three o'clock. I've got that board meeting at five."

"Okay, we'll try for that." Tammy Lyn clicked off the intercom.

Zac wondered how Brianna would phrase her refusal. She'd probably try to poke around in his brain first, wanting to figure out what he hadn't said yesterday. Guilt made him shift uncomfortably.

He hadn't told her his goal of attaining the state job when she'd questioned his reasons for asking for her help. And he should have. Initiating a program to motivate kids that resulted in higher test scores would certainly improve his chances of getting a job developing curriculum, which sounded pretty selfish. But truthfully, influencing education at a state level seemed to Zac the only viable way he could make lasting changes in student achievement, and do it without the people skills he lacked. Still, when Brianna found out state education was his ultimate goal, she would probably assume he was using her.

Aren't you? the nagging little voice in his head demanded.

Yes, he wanted her help to change things in Hope. But her son would benefit from the changes here. So would a lot of other kids. It had been incredibly difficult for Zac to return to the scene of his biggest shame, to the place where he'd spent a year enduring whispers and gossip about their broken relationship. But he'd come back because of the vast changes that were possible here. If only he could engage these kids.

On the surface, seeking Brianna's help seemed stupid. After all, she'd walked out on him, shattered the love he'd had for her when she left him standing at the altar. That love had crumbled to nothing during a year of public humiliation while he fulfilled the teaching contract he'd so stupidly agreed to. But now, ten long years later, they were both back in Hope and the truth was Zac missed the camaraderie they'd once shared when Brianna had been his best friend.

Zac was finished with love. That year in Hope had made him determined to never again take the risk of giving his heart to someone, to never again risk such public humiliation. He'd spent years honing a protective shell that kept anyone from getting too close.

But now he and Brianna lived in the same town, shared the same friends and had a mutual interest in seeing the school do well. Ten years later Zac didn't want her love. He wanted her help.

Persuading her wasn't going to be easy.

"Zac?" Tammy Lyn's intercom voice cracked through his thoughts. "The person you wanted in Las Cruces is out until next week. Sorry. If you could give me that stuff for the board meeting tomorrow I could format it and distribute it today."

"You'll have it as soon as I'm finished," he promised. Mentally steeling himself for Brianna's negative response, Zac blanked out everything and got busy with his notes for the board meeting. They had to be letter perfect because he was lousy at ad-libbing.

Getting that state job would be the culmination of all he'd worked for. That it might ensure nobody in Hope ever said "Poor Zac" again was an added bonus. At state level he could make curriculum more relevant and help kids learn. That was Zac's primary goal.

If he had to do it without Brianna's help, so be it.

Brianna walked up the stairs to the district school office the following afternoon with her throat blocked. This was probably the wrong thing to do. She was a gullible fool. But she was going to do it anyway.

Two minutes later she was seated in Zac's office where he had hot tea and some coconut cookies waiting.

"You're not going to tell me you baked these, are you?" she asked, trying for levity to crack the tension in the air.

"No." He smiled as he poured out two cups. "Sorry."

"Thank you." She accepted her tea, sipped it, inhaling the fresh orangey scent that was her favorite. He'd remembered—another surprise.

"Have a cookie."

Brianna accepted one and chewed on it while he talked about people they knew who were returning for the Homecoming weekend. But eventually the small talk became punctuated by too-long silences. It was time to get to the point.

"I've been thinking a lot about what you said, Zac," she began.

"I shouldn't have asked you." For a brief moment his eyes grew clouded. But then he blinked, and the impassive expression was back in place. "I understand why you have to say no, Brianna. People would talk if we worked together and the gossip—" He rolled his eyes. "Let's just say I don't want to go through that again."

"I'm not concerned about gossip." She frowned.

"Then it's working together that bothers you." Zac rubbed his chin. "I thought—hoped that after so many years we'd be past that and able to concentrate on what's best for the kids, but—"

"It's not the past, either," Brianna sputtered, frustrated that he kept butting in.

"Then it's me. I understand your hesitation." He leaned forward, face earnest. "Forget about it. I'll manage."

"But—"

"No, if you have hesitations, you *should* say no." He sat there, silent, as if he didn't know how to proceed.

"Actually I was going to say yes," she said in her driest tone. "But I think you just talked me out of it. I mean, if you no longer need me—"

Zac's eyes widened. His Adam's apple moved up and down as he gulped. He blinked. "Pardon?"

"I said I would help you. If you want me to." His attitude confused her and she hated feeling confused. "Are you regretting asking for my help, Zac?"

"Uh, no. Not exactly." His carefully blank expression irritated her.

"I know you think I let you down—before." She met his stare. "I won't do that again. I promise."

"This isn't about the past," he murmured.

"Maybe not, but our past certainly weighs into it." She needed to get the guilt out in the open, to deal with it and maybe, finally, be free of it. "You can't deny we have a history."

"I'm not denying anything." His head went up and back, his shoulders straightened. "We made plans." He shrugged. "They didn't happen."

"No. They didn't." Because he and her mother had spoiled that. Suddenly it seemed pointless to discuss the past. "So?" Brianna poured herself another cup of tea just to keep her hands busy. "Where do we start?"

"With Homecoming?" He pulled forward a blank pad and wrote the word across the top in his scratching script. "It would give us the most bang for our buck if we announced a new plan at the Friday-morning assembly. Some parents will probably show up for that so this way they'd learn about our plan at the same time as the kids."

"Whatever our plan is," she added in a droll voice.

"Yeah. Maybe we could put a float in the Homecoming parade." He doodled on the pad.

"A float? We only have a week to organize it. And why a

float? What's the purpose?" Brianna didn't mention that her brain had been whirling with ideas ever since he'd asked her to help, because it was also whirling with confusion at how he'd pushed everything they'd shared into the past. Was it so easy for Zac to forget that he'd once said he loved her?

"Forget about the time left." He leaned back in his chair. "Forget about everything but that some kids need your help. Now, I know you've been thinking about this because you couldn't help yourself. You're compelled to get in there and nurture these kids to do better." He grinned. "So how shall we start?"

They brainstormed ideas. It was slow going at first, but gradually Brianna relaxed enough to let her thoughts roam freely. Finally the idea that had been hidden at the back of her brain burst out.

"Your world." She stared at the scribbles he'd made on the paper, then lifted her head to stare at him. "It's called 'Your World.'"

"Okay." He wrote that down then waited. "Meaning?"

"How do you want your world to look?" She smiled as his face tightened. "That's straight from your lips, Zac. Get kids thinking by giving them a glimpse of what could be, beyond Hope, beyond what is now."

"Good." He tapped his pen. "How do we start?"

"First we need board approval. And a budget. You'll have to get the teachers on board with this, too," she warned.

"I can do that."

She was surprised by how easily Zac accepted her ideas, but she didn't stop to think about it because thoughts kept mushrooming in her head. "Remember Billy Atkins?"

"Billy. Sure, I remember." Zac nodded. "He runs the local newspaper."

"And he's still a phenomenal artist judging by the mural on the side of his building. I think you should have the entry wall, the one you see the moment you enter the school, painted a startling white." She grinned. "And then ask Billy to paint a globe on it with the words *Your World* across the top. Dad could probably help if we needed him."

"Okay." Skepticism filled his face. "What do we do with this globe?"

"This is where you have to be flexible, Zac." She paused, inhaled, then told him the gist of her idea. "Every kid gets a chance to write what he wants to see in his world on that wall." She didn't stop even though his face blanched. "If this is going to work, the students have to believe someone will listen to what they write, listen to what they want. You and the staff must accept their ideas, whether or not you agree with them. You have to be genuine. I will not be part of this if you or the board intend to veto the suggestions they make."

"There are certain things we can't allow," he said stiffly.

"Of course." She nodded. "So you say that to the kids. No vulgarity, no cursing, no inappropriate remarks about teachers. But don't get hung up on the negatives. You want genuine responses that the students are willing to work to achieve."

"And if we get the other?" he asked.

"You have that painted over and wait for a new suggestion." Brianna paused to watch his face. "Be prepared, Zac. It might not go as well as you hope at first. But I think, if given a chance, students will have some remarkable ideas about the way they want their world to look. Some ideas may be quite easy to achieve. But nothing can be discounted just because you think it's too difficult or too far out," she warned. "Every idea deserves consideration."

Zac wrote as fast as she talked, nodding from time to time. When he finally looked at her, a glimmer lit his eyes.

"It might work," he said in a dazed tone. "It just might work."

"It will work, but only if no one judges or criticizes. Your World is all about possibilities."

"What do we do once everyone has contributed?" He laughed and shook his head. "I know what you're going to say. Start working on them. Right?"

"Yes. We'll need a committee of students who are willing to prioritize and a teacher or two who will agree to sit in on their meetings. Sit in on," she repeated firmly. "Not run. This is an initiative by the students."

"Maybe you can think about doing that," he suggested.

Brianna shook her head. "I'm here only to help brainstorm ideas."

"Any more of them?" Zac asked, one eyebrow arched.

"I'd forget about announcing anything at the rally."

"But—" He stopped, looked at her and said, "Go on."

"This might be hard to do in the short time left before Homecoming, but if the board agrees to the plan and you can recruit some people, I think a float in the Homecoming parade is a good idea." He didn't interrupt so she continued. "A great big globe with the words *Your World—How do you see it?* floating down the street will get a lot of attention. No explanation. Nothing. You, the teachers, the board—you all remain silent until the plan is announced on Monday. By the time Monday comes and the wall is ready, everyone in the entire town will be talking."

Zac nodded, jotted a few more things on his paper. By the time he leaned back in his chair, he'd lost the tense air she'd seen when she arrived.

"This is exactly what we need. A little excitement, a little mystery, something out of the ordinary." His eyes met hers sending a little tingle down Brianna's spine.

She was not prepared for his next question.

"Would you be willing to be the spokesperson for Your World at the board meeting?" Zac held up a hand to interrupt her refusal. "You think on your feet. You're good at public speaking. You can present this idea in a way that will grip the board far more than anything I say. They'll listen to you, Brianna."

"They won't listen to you?" She frowned. That didn't sound like a good start.

"Yes, they would. But I'd rather present the information about drugs and the threat to our schools." He met her stare. "I want them to have a clear picture of what could happen if we don't initiate this program."

"You're the negative, I'm the positive, which will make them more inclined to see this as a solution, a way out," she mused. "Good idea."

"You'll do it?"

"Not so fast. By presenting this, I'm the one who'll take the heat if something goes wrong or if the plan fails." She paused. "Or is that the point?"

"I never thought of that, but it works for me." He chuckled at her dark look. "You won't take any heat, Brianna. I'll make sure of that. Anyway, I have a feeling they're going to embrace this idea. It will give everyone a kick start to make changes."

"When's the board meeting?" Brianna asked.

"Tonight."

"What?" She gulped. "Zac, I need time to prepare."

"No, you don't. You always excelled at speaking off the cuff. I doubt that's changed." He stacked his papers together. "Be here at seven. I'll rework the agenda so our plan will go first."

"Zac, I—" Brianna panicked. What was she doing? She hadn't been back in Hope that long. She didn't even know who was on the school board. What business was it of hers to make a suggestion like this to people who'd probably see her as an interloper after so many years?

"Brianna." Zac's hand covered hers and sent a shock-wave up her arm.

"Yes?" She refocused. His dark eyes gleamed with something—hope?

"This is for the kids—for Cory." His fingers tightened against her skin. "Don't think about anything else. Con-centrate on the kids."

Her free hand lifted to touch the outline of her ring lying under the collar of her blouse. The old Zac, the one she'd remembered, had smiled like that and made her think of possibilities, and infused her with courage when she most needed it.

The tingling in her arm magnified. Brianna drew away from his touch. What was it about this man that he could still get her to react with nothing more than a smile and a touch?

"You can do it, Brianna."

There it was again, that encouragement she remembered so well.

"They're just people," he said quietly. "Parents like you who want their kids to succeed. We can help them, if we work together. If we get the town working together."

How many years had she prayed, begged God to let her help kids, to give her the knowledge and grace to make a difference in the world? Her old job had denied her that opportunity. She'd felt useless, a cog in a machine that ground up and spat out those who didn't conform. She'd done her best to help, but this would bring her the chance she'd longed for every time she'd pushed herself a little harder to finish her doctorate. This was why she'd clung to Zac's ring and savored his past words of encouragement even when he was no longer in her life. Now he was telling her she could make a difference in Hope.

"Okay. I'll do it." Her nerves evaporated.

"Thank you."

"On one condition," she added.

"Brianna." Zac sighed. "What condition?"

"Just listen." She had to stand firm on this. "I have Cory, my mom in the nursing home and my dad healing from his heart attack. I also have my work. All of them take my time, time I'll have to cut back on to help you. So I want your agreement that if and when you see a time and place where you can get involved with Cory, you will."

"Cory? But what would I do?" Clearly Zac was not enthralled by the prospect.

"I don't know. But there must be something." Brianna leaned forward. "Cory's on the wrong path and I need help to turn him around before his appointment with the judge at Christmas. I've agreed to help you out, Zac, now I want your promise you'll do what you can to find some common ground with Cory."

"I don't know what I can do," Zac murmured.

"You'll think of something." Inside she was desperately afraid he'd refuse, but she stood firm. "That's my condition, Zac. Take it or leave it." She waited, hoping he'd say yes because she really wanted to be a part of Your World, to make a difference, to see lives changed because of something she'd helped create.

"All right. If there's something I can do, I'll try." That was all Zac said, but it was enough.

His secretary paged him then, so Brianna left. As she drove back to work, she realized Zac's project was her opportunity. If she could just find the right words, share her vision with the school board, maybe she could finally help kids as she'd longed to since she'd left Zac—and this town—so long ago.

"Please don't let me screw this up," Brianna prayed.

Chapter Four

"**D**ad, why is Mom so insistent I revive her store? It's been closed for years." Fresh from a disastrous visit at the nursing home, Brianna flopped into a chair. "I don't understand her obsession with that place."

"Nor did I until last year." Hugh Benson sank into his easy chair, his face sad. "I learned the whole story after a private investigator visited us. You see, your grandfather passed away last year. According to his will, his assets were then distributed to his descendents—Anita being his daughter."

"A grandfather? In Iowa? But you never told me—" Brianna frowned at him.

"I never knew. Your mother told me when we were married that her father was dead. That's all I ever knew until last year when your mother told me her father inherited a furniture store from his father. Anita grew up there. She worked in that store from a very early age, loved it and learned every facet of what went on. You know how adept your mother is at business. As an only child, she expected to one day run the family business herself."

"Of course." Brianna recalled her mother's keen business sense. "She'd have been very good at it. She always had a flair for interior decor."

"Yes." Her father looked grim. "Well, Anita stepped in to manage the place when her dad had his first heart attack. She was only eighteen and did well, except she made a mistake. Her error cost the company money and her father was furious. A little later, when he was forced to retire, he refused to give Anita any control because of that mistake. He said she wasn't smart enough or capable enough to carry on the business he'd inherited from his father."

"Poor Mom. That must have hurt."

"Yes, even more because he put some distant cousin in charge and made Anita one of the hirelings. The cousin made bad mistakes but no matter how Anita pleaded, her father wouldn't recant. Anita was desperately hurt and left Iowa after her mother died. Her father told her not to come back so she didn't. She never spoke to her father again. The bequest he left her was the smallest in his estate, smaller than the least employee's. He punished her to the end."

"So to get back at him, Mom created her own business to pass on to me," Brianna guessed, glimpsing the past with wiser eyes. "That explains so much. But why didn't she ever tell me?"

"Would it have made a difference?" her father asked, his face grave.

"You mean would I have given up my goal of psychology?" she asked. "No. But at least I'd understand why she was so determined that I stay. She was ashamed and embarrassed and determined to prove her father wrong by building her own business. Except I couldn't be part of it." Hindsight explained a lot.

"So now you know." Hugh Benson's pencil flew across the page, his caricature of Cory coming to life. "You said you came back to Hope to help kids. So that's why you're helping Zac present this Your World plan tonight?"

"Yes." Brianna sighed. "I'm not sure about working with him, though."

"Because?"

But Brianna could not, dare not answer that. Not until she'd sorted out the miasma of conflicting feelings that took over whenever Zac was around.

Outside, a short beep of a car horn sounded.

"That's Jaclyn. We're going out for a quick supper before I go to the board meeting. I know you're going back to see Mom. Cory's eating at his new friend's house but he's supposed to be back in a couple of hours." Brianna grabbed her bag and her jacket. As she slipped her feet out of slippers and into her sandals she felt her dad's stare. "What?"

"I thought—hoped you might stop by the nursing home later tonight. You know the truth now. Maybe you two could make up." There was no condemnation in his quiet voice but that didn't stop Brianna feeling a ripple of guilt.

"It's too soon for that, Dad." She grabbed the doorknob. "Mom was pretty upset today." She winced, remembering her mother's angry diatribe.

"Brianna." Her dad's firm tone insisted she hear him out.

She inhaled and waited.

"Your mother had a stroke." He sounded angry. "She can't do the things she wants to do and her temper flares. She gets uncertain mood swings and frequently can't express herself the way she wants. Cut her some slack, will you?"

All the past hurt, all the angry words and bitter remarks she'd endured came flooding back. Brianna couldn't stop the rush of anger.

"I've been cutting Mom slack my whole life, Dad. I figured that maybe, after all these years, she might have learned to do the same for her one and only daughter. But I guess I still embarrass her." Stung by the chastisement in his eyes, she left, quietly but firmly shutting the door behind her before she walked to her friend's car.

"Hey, Brianna. I'm starv—" Jaclyn took one look at her face and turned off the car. "What's wrong? Cory again?" She frowned, shook her head. "No, wait. I know that look. It's your mom, isn't it, Brianna?"

"I'm a fully accredited psychologist, Jaclyn. I've dealt with all kinds of people. Yet, I can't seem to deal with my feelings toward my own mother." Slowly she unclenched her fingers as she relayed what she'd learned. "It explains why, all these years, she's been so driven. But why couldn't she have just told me?"

"Old grudges die hard." Jaclyn frowned. "Now, what are you going to do about it?"

"Keep trying to rebuild our relationship." Brianna couldn't keep the bitterness of the past inside any longer; she had to let it out. "My mother is the reason I left Hope. Well, her and Zac."

"I'm your best friend, Brianna." Jaclyn frowned. "Isn't it about time you finally explained why I never got to wear your mother's choice of that delightful flounced fuchsia bridesmaid dress down the aisle for your wedding?" She giggled at Brianna's gagging sound but quickly sobered. "You're only about ten years late explaining."

"It was always too hard to talk about. I wanted to forget it." She gulped, forced herself to continue the sad story. "Remember the rehearsal dinner?"

"Like I could forget that—all eleven courses." Jaclyn grimaced.

"There weren't eleven!" Brianna argued. "But my mother did have to make her only daughter's wedding an extravaganza."

"Go on."

"After the rehearsal dinner I hadn't seen Zac for a while so I went looking for him. He and my mother were by the hotel pool." Brianna bit her lip. "I overheard them talking. He accepted her offer of a teaching job in Hope for two years. Without even talking to me, he accepted."

"But how could—?" Jaclyn's furrowed brow smoothed. "Oh, I remember now. Your mom was elected chairman of the school board that year, wasn't she?"

"Yes. And she had the store, of course." Brianna swallowed hard. "I heard Zac tell her he was worried about supporting me. Remember I couldn't find a job that summer. As my mother said many times, I returned to Hope with a useless undergrad degree." Bitterness ate another hole inside.

"She never understood how much psychology meant to you, did she?"

"She always said I should get over Jessica's death, like it was a skinned knee or something." Brianna bit her lip. "It hurt so badly to lose her. I couldn't just forget her or that her death might have been prevented if better medical care had been available in Hope."

"Nor could I," Jaclyn murmured.

"Anyway that night Mom preyed on Zac's fears." Brianna needed to get this out and let go of it. "She convinced Zac we should stay in Hope by guaranteeing him a job and telling him that I'd have work in her store while he taught. She said we'd be able to save faster for our PhDs."

"Baloney." Jaclyn snorted. "She was always after you to take over her store. She couldn't accept your refusal so she decided to bribe your fiancé to get her way."

"Exactly. I couldn't believe Zac agreed with her that I should work in the store. He knew as well as you did how useless I felt in that place. I was never into home decor. I had no knack for furniture styles or placement. Still don't,"

Brianna admitted. "The only thing I enjoyed about that store was the fabrics, hence my love of quilts."

"Did you talk to Zac about it?"

"I tried on the way home after the party. I asked why he'd accepted the job without talking to me. He was surprised that I was angry about it. He thought I'd be glad that we wouldn't have to go into a lot of debt for our degrees." She squeezed her eyes tightly shut and inhaled to ease the stress of those horrible moments. "He said I'd probably end up reconsidering my decision to do a doctorate anyway once we had a family."

"Shades of male machismo." Jaclyn's face tightened.

"No. He wasn't being macho. I don't think he honestly believed I was as committed as he was." Brianna sighed. "I was stunned by what he said. Weeks of him falling in with my mother's suggestions and not standing up for me—I'd been having doubts about getting married and I told him so. But he apologized, convinced me that he loved me, that he only wanted what was best for us."

"So you decided to go through with the wedding."

"Yes. But I was furious. When I got home, I told my mother I knew she'd gone behind my back to coerce Zac into accepting that job." Brianna tried to make her friend understand. "She knew we'd planned to get jobs in the city where we could still take night classes because I'd gone to great lengths to explain our plans to my parents. Zac and I had put months of thought into it because I'd insisted we have our game plan in place before we ever came to Hope for the wedding. She knew that plan and she deliberately ruined it."

Jaclyn squeezed her shoulder in sympathy. "Tell me the rest."

"Eventually my mother admitted asking Zac's mom to say she was too ill to travel for the wedding so we'd have to come here to get married. It was all part of her plan. Zac and I, we were just pawns."

There was nothing Jaclyn could say.

"I asked her why she'd done it. Do you know what she said?" The protective barrier she'd maintained for so many years was breached as tears welled. Brianna made no attempt to stop them. "My mother claimed she'd done it to help me. She said Zac told her he was worried I'd never be able to support myself, that he felt I was holding him back. She said Zac's mom was afraid I might derail his goal to get his PhD. My mother insisted she couldn't stand by and watch me lose him. The way she put it, I began to believe she was right, that for Zac's sake I needed to stay and work in the store."

"Oh, Brianna. I wish you'd called me."

"I wish I had, too. But I was so confused. And Mom just kept piling it on. I was a weight on Zac's back, but she said she would rescue me. She would make me assistant manager at her store. I'd run things and she'd take a break once in a while."

"That wouldn't have happened. She always had to be the boss." Jaclyn bit her lip. "Sorry."

"Don't be. It's true." Brianna swallowed. "Anyway, she said I had to prove to Zac that I didn't need him to be responsible for me, so he wouldn't feel I was—let's see, 'a chain around his neck' was the way she put it. She said that maybe then he wouldn't resent me."

Jaclyn made a face. "And Zac? You did talk to him about it?"

"After my argument with my mother I called him. He said she was right, that he had been worried but he wasn't now that he had the job. He said it was better to stay in Hope and save." Brianna pursed her lips. "He even suggested we consider moving in with one or the other of our parents to cut costs further."

Jaclyn groaned.

"I was reeling." Brianna tried to smile. "All our plans were out the window. I just wanted him to reassure me. But Zac was really worried about the financial aspect of both of us returning to school. He even said he was glad I was willing to do my share. As if I was some kind of leech!"

"He was probably just nervous. Zac was never great with words," Jaclyn reminded.

"He repeated over and over that he was glad I'd *finally* be working," Brianna sputtered. "And he kept babbling about getting his PhD as soon as possible. He sounded as if he thought I'd ask him to give up his dream."

"He used to bore us to tears with that PhD dream sometimes, didn't he? But I'm sure he loved you," Jaclyn consoled.

"Well, I wasn't so sure. And the more my mother talked to me, the less sure I became. She played me like a fiddle, Jaclyn." Brianna sighed. "I finally decided she was right, that I was holding back the man I loved and that I needed to give up my own dream to help Zac. So I agreed to work in her store."

Jaclyn frowned. "But you didn't stay, Brianna. You left."

"Yes." Brianna couldn't stop her tears. A bitter smile rose from the cauldron of bitterness simmering inside. "Zac phoned me the next morning to tell me of my mother's suggestion that we cut our honeymoon short so I could start work early, as thanks for the elaborate wedding that I never wanted."

Jaclyn's face expressed her disgust.

"I told him in no uncertain terms what I thought of that. He sounded hurt. He was only trying to help make it easier for me, he said. It would be a sacrifice but sometimes sacrifices were necessary. I told him I felt I was making all the sacrifices and he said that he was sacrificing, too, by having to put off his doctorate. We argued a bit, made up and I hung up. Then my mother appeared with a list she'd made of my future duties and responsibilities at the store and a contract."

"A contract?" Jaclyn lifted one eyebrow.

"She said I'd need to sign a contract for five years to make sure she wasn't left high and dry if I changed my mind. Five years!" Brianna straightened her shoulders. "I knew then how it would be, how she'd grind me down until I gave up my plan to become a child psychologist. And I knew Zac wouldn't be strong enough to stand up to her, either. You see she was right about one thing."

"Right how?" Jaclyn glared at her. "Explain."

"I'd been worried for some time that I was holding Zac back. He was so much smarter, had so much to offer. I slowed him down because he spent so much time helping me, time he should have spent on his own work." Brianna dashed away her tears. "If we'd married and I got stuck in her store, Zac would have felt compelled to stay those five years, too. I didn't want him to lose his dream because of me."

"That woman!" Jaclyn sputtered.

"It wasn't just Mom." Brianna felt the weight of it dragging her down. Wasn't confession supposed to make her feel better? "By then Zac was completely under her spell, convinced that giving up our plans to teach in Hope was his opportunity. I was afraid Zac would eventually turn against me if I objected too much and I couldn't stand that. I loved him and I wanted him to be happy. I thought he would be if I wasn't there so I packed a bag and snuck away."

"I would have helped you if I'd known."

"I know. But then Mom would have caused problems for you." Brianna paused. "Dad saw me leave."

"Really?"

"When I was in the cab, I looked back and saw him standing there. He was crying." Brianna dabbed at her wet cheeks with the tissue Jaclyn handed her. "I wrote him later that when I did get married I'd make sure he walked me down the aisle, but that didn't happen. After Craig proposed, he insisted we marry quickly. He was sick and he wanted me to be able to stay at his house and care for Cory without any improprieties. I was afraid my mother would talk me out of it if she knew, so I married Craig with nobody there. But Craig betrayed me, too."

"How?" Jaclyn asked, her beautiful face sad.

"Craig died three months after we married. That's when I learned he'd known all along that he had a terminal illness." Brianna stared through the windshield remembering the gut-wrenching dismay when she learned the truth. "He knew he didn't have long to live, but he never told me. He pretended he was getting better. Maybe he thought I would have left if I'd known."

Jaclyn's hand covered hers and squeezed.

"I wouldn't have left," Brianna whispered. "Craig was wonderful to me in those horrible weeks after I left Hope for Chicago. He took time to help me find a place to live, helped me find a job. Cory was Craig's pride and joy but neither he nor his first wife, Cory's mother, had family. He had no one to help him. He adored that boy but I saw how hard it became for him to care for him. I wanted to help because I loved Cory, too."

"But you didn't love Craig?"

"No." Brianna smiled, sadness filling her heart. "I wish I could have. He was a wonderful man. But there was never love between us. We were just good friends who married a few months after we met to give Cory a home. At least I thought that's what we were. But when I learned the truth, that he knew—" Brianna bit her lip. "I might not have been so decimated if Craig had prepared me. But he never said a word and suddenly at twenty-three I was a widow and a mother, responsible for this little boy, no clue how I was going to do it and all alone. I was at my lowest when I phoned you for help."

"I'm glad you finally did. That's what friends are for." She wrapped her arms around Brianna and help on tight. "I wish I could have come."

"I know. But you sent your mother instead, and she was wonderful to me. I'll never be able to thank her or you enough." Brianna clung a moment longer then drew back. "Anyway, all of this was to say my dad razzed me about going to see Mom tonight."

"You should go," Jaclyn insisted.

"I can't go to the nursing home again," Brianna admitted. "Not for a while."

"Why not?"

"Today she said I made her ashamed." The lump in Brianna's stomach hardened. "It hurt so much. I don't want to live with that pain again, Jaclyn. I'm done with trying to be the obedient daughter I'm supposed to be. It didn't work for her and it doesn't work for me." Briefly Brianna explained what she'd learned about her grandfather.

"I understand." Jaclyn reached out and started the car. She shifted into gear before facing Brianna. "But you can't go on hating her, either. You've got to find a way past it. And you've got to do the same with Zac. Didn't you say he wanted you to work with him?"

"He's got this idea that I can help him shake up the school."

"About time that school had a good shake-up," Jaclyn

said, steering into the restaurant parking lot. "Couldn't hurt your career to be at the forefront of change, either, could it?"

"No," Brianna mumbled.

"Then?" Jaclyn lifted an eyebrow. "What's the problem?"

"The truth?" Brianna climbed out of the car.

"Always."

"I don't know if I can work with Zac." That admission wasn't easy.

"You probably can't," Jaclyn agreed, walking with her to the front door. "Until you let go of your resentment of him. You were young. You both made mistakes because you didn't trust each other. It will take some heavenly healing and help for you to start again, Bri." She rolled her eyes. "Listen to me—the pediatrician advising the child psychologist."

"No, the best friend advising her dim-witted school buddy. Thanks, pal." She stopped Jaclyn before they went inside and hugged her. "Did I tell you I'm so happy you and Kent are having a baby?"

"Me, too. But I want you to be happy, too, Brianna. And you aren't going to be until you make peace with the past. So think about it. Okay?" She waited for her friend's nod. "And I'll pray for you to find a way to mend things with your mom. And Zac." Then Jaclyn tugged her inside the café where they chose their favorite Mexican food.

Brianna enjoyed the meal. But her thoughts kept straying to Zac.

Would the past interfere with working together?

When Jaclyn dropped her off at Zac's office, she went inside only after whispering a prayer for the right words, and after reminding herself that she was doing this for Cory, not Zac.

Chapter Five

Later that night Zac rapped on Brianna's front door, excitement zinging through him. She opened the door, her hair tousled, her feet bare, her face weary.

"We got it," he said simply. "Your World is a go."

Her smile dawned slowly, starting in her eyes, which glowed green in the cast of the house light. The grin moved to light up her entire face, transforming her weariness into beauty.

"Come in, Zac." She waved him to a chair, then flopped down on the sofa across from him and tucked her long legs under her. Her eyes sparkled. "So? Tell me what happened after I left."

"Lots of good discussion." Zac glanced around, remembering how the expensive knickknacks in this living room had always seemed to get in the way of his gangly teenage elbows and feet. Most of them were gone now rendering the room less glamorous but immensely more homey.

"Meaning?" Brianna leaned forward impatiently. "Did they approve everything?"

"Yes." He grinned, sharing the success. "Your speech was brilliant, by the way, especially the part about saving money in the long run. There was so much interest, I had to caution several board members to keep the plan quiet for now."

"Good."

He explained the budget that had been allocated and told her the few worries he'd heard.

"It all sounds quite positive," Brianna said, then frowned. "Oh, do you want some coffee? Or something?"

"I'm coffee-ed out, thanks." Silence stretched between them, leaving Zac feeling as he had the first time he'd come here—awkward. Nothing new about that feeling. He opened his mouth to rehash more details of the meeting but Brianna spoke first.

"So Your World is on its way." She nibbled her bottom lip, studying him from beneath her lashes.

"Yep."

"And Cory? Did you think of anything you could do with Cory?" Her eyes stretched wide with expectation.

"Not yet." Zac felt like a heel because he hadn't actually given it a thought. He'd been too busy concentrating on that board meeting. "What is it you expect?" he asked cautiously.

The telephone interrupted her response. Brianna picked it up, her face losing its joy as a querulous voice cut across the peace that had filled the room.

"It's quite late, Mom. Are you sure—yes, yes, okay. I'll bring it right away," she promised. She hung up the phone, tense lines marring the beauty of her face. "I have to go out."

"Now?" he asked. A sound on the stairs drew their attention. In a second her face changed, that sad hurt transformed into a mask of unconcern.

"It's okay, Dad. Go back to bed. Mom can't sleep. She wants me to bring over a pattern. She's really getting into this knitting thing, isn't she?" She smiled at him. "I think it will probably help strengthen her hands. Since the stroke she's had problems."

"Hello, Zac." Greetings exchanged, Mr. Benson turned back to Brianna. "You don't want me to go?"

"No. I'll do it. Cory's in his room, in bed I hope, so nothing to worry about there. I won't be long." She waited until he nodded and left, then she turned to face Zac. "I'm sorry. I'd like to talk to you more about Cory, but I have to go to the nursing home."

"Okay." The slide of emotions across her face bothered him. For some reason he didn't understand Zac knew he couldn't let her go alone. "I'll go with you."

"You?" She blinked. "Why?" she asked simply.

"I need to do something to wind down." He shrugged. "If you don't want me to go with you, I can always go for a run I guess."

"Actually, I'd be glad if you came." Relief made the gold sparkles in her eyes glitter. "I'll have to find the pattern she wants first, though."

"Maybe I can help." He followed her to her mother's office but jerked to a halt in the doorway, remembering the one time Mrs. Benson had found them studying in here and the angry scolding she'd laid on Brianna.

"It should be—yes, here it is." She removed a piece of paper from a file, copied it on a nearby copier and slid the original back into its folder in a drawer. The drawer slid shut without a sound.

"I wish my home office was this neat," he said, studying the immaculate room. "This looks like a show place."

"That's because no one uses it." Brianna glanced around.

"Why not? As I remember you always loved to do craft stuff."

"Not in here. This is my mother's room." A pained look

washed across her face before she glanced away. "I'm ready."

Once he'd handed her into his car, Zac quickly drove to the nursing home and parked in the empty spot nearest the door. They walked inside without speaking, but he couldn't help thinking what a shame it was that the bright room with its many windows was still off-limits to Brianna.

Zac spotted Miss Latimer, his mother's old friend, sitting in her wheelchair. To give Brianna privacy with her mom he told her he'd catch up with her in a minute.

"Hey, Miss Latimer. How are you?" Zac bent over so the old woman's cataract-covered eyes could see him.

She inhaled, blinked and her face creased in a huge smile. His heart felt a burst of warmth that even though his mother was gone, someone was glad to see him.

"I'm very well, Zachary." She patted his hand. "Thank you for asking. You're rather late tonight. A board meeting?"

"Yes. How do you keep up on all the goings on in Hope?" he asked, amazed as usual by her sharp memory.

"Clean living." She winked at him, then launched into a tale of the most recent happenings in the nursing home.

Zac tried to focus on what she was saying but it grew steadily more difficult because of the racket coming from a room down the hall.

"Isn't it dreadful? She's horrid to that girl," Miss Latimer murmured, leaning close.

"Who's horrid to whom?" he asked.

"Anita Benson is horrible to her daughter, Brianna."

"Oh." He tried to pretend he couldn't hear the vitriolic comments.

"That woman has always ridden roughshod over other people's feelings, but lately she's grown worse. Poor Brianna can't do anything right."

"I guess it's part of her stroke issues," Zac temporized, shrinking at what he heard.

"Huh! Anita uses that as an excuse for her poor behavior." Miss Latimer snorted her disgust. "She was always a bully, but nobody's ever had the courage to say it to her face." She stopped and pursed her lips as a diatribe of complaints echoed down the hall. "Poor girl."

A harried nurse raced toward the room but soon came scurrying back out, her face flushed and her lips in a tight angry line. Zac cringed as those few residents still about stared. Poor Brianna.

"Maybe there's something I can do," he said quietly.

"By all means, Zachary, go." She squeezed his hand. "Brianna's such a sweet girl. It's too bad she's always had such a difficult time with her mother."

She had? Zac didn't remember that. Back in the old days, Mrs. Benson had always been very nice to him, though now he thought about it, they hadn't gone to Brianna's elegant home to study very often. He couldn't remember why.

"We'll visit another time," Miss Latimer promised.

"Yes, we will." He squeezed her hand. After a moment's thought he stopped to buy something at the gift shop that was just closing then strode down the hall, battling his nervousness as he broached the room. This was none of his business. But he felt sorry for Brianna.

"Mother, stop making a scene. This *is* the pattern you asked for," Brianna said calmly.

Zac tapped his knuckles against the open door then stuck his head inside. With her hands clenched at her side, he guessed Brianna was anything but calm.

"Hello, Mrs. Benson." He walked in, pulled the small box of saltwater taffy from his jacket pocket and held it out to the red-faced woman. "I brought you a gift."

"A gift? Oh, you lovely man." Mrs. Benson reached out

and took the package. "I love sweets. Now that's the kind of thing you should have thought of," she said, tossing a glare at her daughter.

"No more visiting tonight, Mrs. Benson." The nurse stepped into the room and held the door, motioning for them to leave.

"I guess we have to go now. I'll see you tomorrow, Mom." Brianna ushered Zac out the door while the sticky taffy she was chewing prevented Anita Benson from arguing. "Thank you, Zac," she murmured once they were in the hall. Her lashes fanned across her embarrassed pink cheeks. "I—uh—" The words died away as her cheeks grew even pinker.

"Not a problem," he said. "Anyway I had a chance to say hi to Miss Latimer. Remember her?"

"Math." Brianna cast a quick look around, obviously relieved when she didn't spot her former teacher. "My worst subject. Oh, yes, I remember her."

"I loved math." Zac shrugged at her glower as they walked across the parking lot. "Well I did. Miss Latimer was such a great friend to my mom during her illness that it's my pleasure to visit her whenever I can." He unlocked the car, held the door until she was seated inside.

Zac walked around the car, searching for another subject. "I recognized that deep, rich blue of your father's in the painting in your mom's room. Nobody else gets it quite that shade."

"Yes." Brianna smiled. "The smaller one beside it is Cory's."

"I didn't realize he painted." Zac had been surprised by the delicate touch of the watercolor of Mrs. Benson caught in a happy moment.

"He didn't but Dad's been coaching him." Brianna fell silent.

"He's a good teacher." Zac studied Brianna, noting she'd inherited her mother's amazing eyes, though Brianna's now looked infinitely tired. The confrontation with her mother seemed to have drained her. He pressed a little harder on the accelerator to get her home more quickly. "How is Cory doing?"

"He's made some friends I'm not too keen on," she mumbled. "They've eaten at our house for the past three nights. Not that I care about that, but they never seem to go home unless I tell them to. It's odd."

"Sounds like it." Zac wondered if they were the source of the drugs.

"Day after tomorrow is the Homecoming parade," Brianna reminded him. "Is the float ready?" Her gorgeous eyes narrowed when he didn't immediately answer. He avoided her searching gaze. "It's not finished," she said with disgust.

"I'm working on it." Zac's frustration at his ineptitude with that stupid float surged.

"So what's the problem?" Brianna demanded as he pulled into her driveway.

"If I knew that, I'd fix it. I don't know," he admitted. He got out, met her at the hood of his car.

"Zac!" Brianna's eyes shot daggers. "The Your World project depends on kicking off with that float. I thought you agreed."

"I do. It's just—I'm not mechanically inclined, Brianna. The globe won't balance." Annoyed, Zac followed her to the front door, waited while she unlocked it.

"You're the one who asked me for help, Zac. If you don't want to do this—" She left it hanging, as if he'd deliberately messed up.

"I *do* want to do it. I just don't know how." He'd been going to leave but instead followed her inside to defend himself, forcing his tone to stay even though inside he fumed at the way she'd turned this on him. "Maybe we have to go with a smaller idea."

"So my idea is at fault. That's what you always did when something didn't work the way you wanted. You blamed me." Brianna's glare would have put a frost on the desert.

"I'm not blaming anyone." Zac inhaled and let it out slowly, searching for a way through this minefield. "I'm just telling you that I've had some problems." He tried to explain the issues with keeping the globe spinning but quickly gave up. Sometimes being a nerd was absolutely worthless. "I don't really know anything about making a globe spin," he admitted.

"Then why on earth did you agree—"

"Hey, do I need to put on my referee suit?" Cory, sprawled on the sofa, flicked on a lamp, a half sneer on his face. "What's going on?"

"Nothing," Brianna said, her voice sharp. "You're supposed to be in bed."

"The float for the Homecoming parade is what's going on, Cory." Zac raised an eyebrow at Brianna. "It's not that big a secret," he said. He turned to Cory. "Unfortunately when it comes to the mechanics of fixing things, I am a complete moron."

"Maybe I could help." Cory glanced at his mother.

"Oh, son, I don't—"

The little sparkle of excitement that had flickered in Cory's eyes for a fraction of a second snuffed out. Zac had to intervene.

"Maybe you could help, Cory," he agreed. "I'm pretty sure there's a short somewhere. How are you with wiring?" He ignored Brianna's attempts to catch his eye. "How about tomorrow after school? Could you take a look then?"

"I guess." Cory risked a second look at Brianna. "If Mom's okay with it."

"Why wouldn't she be? She just finished nagging me to get the thing going." Zac ignored Brianna's tightened lips and hiss of anger. "I'll pick you up after the last class. Okay?"

"Sure." Cory rose. "I'd better get to bed. Don't fight anymore, Mom." He winked at Zac before he took the stairs to his room two at a time.

"What are you doing?" Brianna demanded in a low voice.

"I'm trying to help Cory. Did you see the way his eyes lit up when he offered to help?" Zac touched her arm. "He wants to do it, Brianna. If he can't, I'll find someone else, but he was being generous offering his help. At least give him the chance. Besides, it will keep him away from those friends of his you don't like. For a bit, anyway."

Brianna was quiet for a long while, her hazel eyes studying him. Finally she nodded.

"Maybe you're right," she murmured with a sigh. "Maybe I've made him feel unneeded by trying to protect him too much. Maybe I should have included him more."

"Brianna." Zac touched her shoulder, his fingers tingling at the warmth of her skin. "Don't beat yourself up about this. You're a mom and you naturally try to protect your kid."

"Yes, but—" She bit her lip, her face troubled. "I'm not sure—"

"You asked me to do something with him," he reminded. "So let me try this. At the very least we'll get to know each other a little better." Zac drew his hand away, surprised by his yearning to wrap his arm around Brianna's shoulder and draw her close, to comfort her and erase the worry etched on her face. "Trust me."

Brianna didn't say she trusted him.

All she said was, "Tomorrow after school, then. Don't forget."

Zac said good-night and walked out to his car, speculating on exactly why he'd offered to help Cory. Maybe seeing how Mrs. Benson's tirade had deflated Brianna made him want to ease her world a little. It was embarrassing how much Brianna Benson still affected him.

The woman had talked to him on the phone on their wedding day mere minutes before she'd left town without a single word of explanation! And now she had him in knots again with crazy feelings he didn't understand and couldn't seem to control.

Irritated, discomfited and frustrated by his topsy-turvy reactions, Zac grit his teeth when he heard her call his name. He stopped and turned, one hand on the door handle of his car.

"I just wanted— You look kind of green, Zac." Brianna peered into his face. "Something you ate?"

If only a remedy was that simple. Take an antacid and get rid of this ridiculous response to her.

"Zac?"

Worry filled her pretty face. That was the most special thing about Brianna. Always concerned about everyone. Heart of gold. Which is probably why her mother's repudiation wounded her so deeply. If only he could— Zac regrouped.

"I'm fine. Did you forget something?" He was determined not to fall into the same old habit of wanting more than he knew he could have. Brianna was nothing but an old friend.

That wouldn't, couldn't change, because he couldn't let it. The shame of the past had ensured that.

"I just wanted to say thanks." Brianna reached out but her hand froze midair. She licked her lips as if she had second thoughts. "For going with me to the nursing home."

"You're welcome." When she said no more, Zac climbed

in his car and drove to his lonely house where he sat in the dark, struggling to make sense of what had just happened.

Why was it that the beautiful woman he'd once proposed to, the one who'd run away rather than marry him, still only had to smile to make him start dreaming about what ifs? Hadn't he learned anything in ten years?

There was no point asking God for relief. If Zac had learned one thing in all those years, he'd learned God didn't have time to be bothered with his insecurities. So he kept his mask of invincibility intact. He wasn't the kind of person who could open up, reveal the pain she'd caused and ask for an explanation. That vulnerability risked getting hurt and Zac wasn't about to go there.

Brianna was off-limits as anything more than a colleague and maybe a friend.

Losing everything they'd shared hurt, but Zac figured that God must want it that way or He'd have changed things. That nothing had changed, told Zac he was still a cog that didn't fit in God's wheel.

"This was a great idea, Brianna." Zac flashed her a grin as he filled another bowl with chips. "Getting us all together after Homecoming, I mean."

"Thanks. But I couldn't have done it if you hadn't picked up snacks. Today was wild in my office." She ignored the way his smile made her pulse skitter and concentrated on refilling the cheese tray.

"Homecoming is usually a crazy time for everyone." Zac reached in front of her, speared a cube of cheese and popped it in between his lips.

"Speaking of Homecoming—" Kent leaned against the doorjamb "—awesome job with the float, guys. I had a hundred people ask me what Your World means."

"That's exactly what we want, anticipation building until

all is revealed on Monday." Brianna shared a look with Zac but quickly looked away.

"We have Cory, his friends and their dads to thank that the float operated at all." Zac inclined his head.

She noticed her son looming on the bottom step and stifled her misgivings. His friends? Brianna hadn't realized Zac had so much help.

"You did a great job. Thank you, son."

"You're welcome." Cory grinned at Kent. "It was a pretty easy fix. I wouldn't ask him—" he inclined his head in Zac's direction "—to work on your truck, though. Mechanics aren't his strength."

"Dude, I so already knew that." Kent smirked at Zac as he high-fived Cory.

"Are you going out?" Brianna asked her son with a quick glance at the clock.

"Yeah. I'm meeting the guys at the café." Cory's brows lowered as if he expected her to object.

"Have fun. And be home on time," she reminded, refusing to mention his curfew aloud.

"Yes, Mother." The door slammed behind him.

"Hey. Did the party move in here?" Nick Green, their friend who'd turned his quarterback skills into a professional career in the NFL strolled into the kitchen. He looked around, shook his head and grabbed the bowl of chips. "Not enough room," he said before he disappeared into the family room.

"Hey, Nick, hold up. I want to know how you came up with that last play of the game. It was pretty slick," Kent said, leaving the room.

Brianna watched through the windows as Cory greeted his friends. After a quick backward glance at her he hurried away.

Lord, please keep him safe.

"Brianna—"

"Yes?" Zac's touch on her arm jerked her back to awareness. She flinched at the spark his touch engendered and saw him blink.

"Sorry." He stepped back.

"It's okay." She forced a smile. "I guess I zoned out for a minute."

"Brianna, what's wrong?" Zac glanced from the window to her. "Did Cory do something?"

"Not that I know of. Yet." She picked up the tray she'd been arranging, wishing she had avoided these moments alone with Zac.

"I want to thank Cory for his help with the float in a concrete way. Would it be okay if he came for dinner one night? Kent comes over most Wednesdays when Jaclyn works late. I usually barbecue steaks." Zac blinked. "Would Cory like that?"

"You don't have to invite him." But she was glad he'd offered. Maybe Zac could get Cory to take an interest in something other than the two boys he called friends. "But, yes, I'm sure he'd love a good steak. I don't cook it often because I'm not good at grilling."

Was this the help for her son that she'd been praying for? A Proverbs verse she'd memorized in youth group long ago flickered through her mind. *If you falter in times of trouble, how small is your strength.* It seemed she was constantly faltering, and her strength was diminishing with every day.

"He's going to be okay, Brianna." Zac had moved to stand behind her and now his breath brushed her ear. "Cory's nobody's fool. Relax. Give him a chance to prove himself."

"Have some faith. Is that what you mean?" She smiled, nodded and motioned toward the other room. "I'll try. Let's go catch up on what everyone's been doing."

Brianna pretended to enjoy the rest of the evening. She listened to her old friends tease one another, found out their friend Shay expected to return to Hope within six months and realized that Nick wasn't just her old pal anymore. He, like Shay, was famous, though unlike her, he seemed unchanged by it. Shay seemed much more reserved, and she wondered why, but Brianna's thoughts kept returning to Cory.

One by one her friends eventually left after thanking her for the evening. Zac remained behind to help with clean-up. When he caught her glancing at the clock for the third time in five minutes he took the dishes from her hand, put them in the dishwasher then turned her to face him.

"What time was Cory supposed to be home?"

"An hour ago." She could hide her worry no longer. "He's not supposed to break his curfew, Zac. That's one of the judge's conditions."

"Cory knows that. He'll be here soon." Though kind, his words did nothing to comfort her.

"He's never broken it before by more than a couple of minutes." Brianna stared at him, knowing she had to ask, but wishing it was someone else. Anyone else. She did not want to need Zac. Yet she did. "Will you help me look for him? Please?"

"Sure." There was no hesitation. Zac grabbed his jacket and his keys. "We can take my car."

"Just let me tell Dad what we're doing so he can phone me if he hears from Cory." Relief made her feel light-headed as Brianna raced up the stairs and explained to her dad. She returned to find Zac had finished the cleaning. Everything sparkled. "You didn't have to do that."

"No big deal. Ready?" He handed her into his car.

They drove all over town but found no sign of Cory or his friends.

"It's after midnight," she said. Panic lurked in the back of her throat. "Something's wrong."

"Nothing in town is open now," Zac agreed. "Hope isn't exactly a night spot. Maybe they went out of town."

"For what?" Brianna heard the anger in her voice and modulated it. This wasn't Zac's fault. "I don't know why they would do that, but I guess we can check." She was bowed down with the knowledge that this child she had promised Craig she'd protect was in trouble.

Ten minutes later the headlights of Zac's car caught three figures trudging toward town. Anger vied for relief. As soon as Zac pulled to the side of the road, Brianna reached for the door handle.

"Brianna." Zac's hand on her shoulder stopped her. "I know I have no business telling you this, but I'm going to say it anyway. Don't yell at Cory in front of his friends, even though he deserves it. You can bawl him out later. For now, just listen."

She glared at him, but she knew he was right. Cory would only be embarrassed if she did the mom thing in front of his friends, and they didn't need any more conflicts to add to the strain already building between them. She'd wait until they were home.

Brianna inhaled and opened the door. The trio stood next to the right front fender. Cory looked at her with a mixture of shame and a tinge of defiance. The other two acted nonchalant.

"Need a ride?" It cost Brianna a great deal not to embrace Cory, so great was her relief at seeing him healthy and alive.

"Yeah. Thanks, Mom." He got in the backseat with his two friends. "Thanks, Mr. Ender. We would have never all fit in Mom's little car."

"What were you doing out here?" Zac asked after a sideways glance at Brianna. He turned around and headed back to Hope as the kids explained that they'd hitchhiked out to an old mine they'd heard about.

"But by the time we were ready to come back, we couldn't catch a ride. Seems like everything around Hope dies at night." That was Adam, the kid Brianna had dubbed the ringleader. His tone was scathing. "Where I come from there's life after nine."

"Where is that?" Zac asked.

"L.A. Man, that place always has something to offer."

"We'll drop you at home," Brianna said. "Where do you live?" The two boys argued to be dropped off in the middle of town but Brianna refused, insisting they be left at home. She heaved a huge sigh of relief when the two were gone and glanced at Cory, expecting an explanation. But his head was down. Probably embarrassed in front of Zac. He should be. She vacillated between anger and relief.

Zac drove them home, saying nothing to break the silence. Brianna waited until he'd pulled into her driveway.

"Go inside, Cory. Wait for me in the living room." She looked straight at him, expecting an argument. Cory said nothing, simply got out of the car, thanked Zac and went inside. Brianna turned to Zac. "Thank you for your help. I really appreciate it. I would never have thought—"

He chuckled and shook his head. "I guess you have to be a guy to think of some things. Don't worry about it. I was happy to help. I'm just glad we found Cory safe and sound."

"Yes." Her fingers curled against the door handle. She needed to get out of this intimate atmosphere before she said something she'd regret. "Just let me know when you want Cory to come over for dinner, will you?" She pushed open the door and met his gaze. "And thank you. Again."

"My pleasure. And thank you for the party. It was good to see everyone again." Zac looked confident, competent and totally in control.

Everything Brianna was not. But, then, Zac didn't have a son to raise.

"Well, good night." She closed the door and walked inside the house, praying desperately for heavenly help with a situation she felt incapable of handling. "Please, God, give me the words to say to Cory."

Another verse popped into her head.

You will keep Him in perfect peace whose mind is fixed on You.

Was that what she was doing wrong? Not spending enough time focusing on God?

Tonight, right after she read the riot act to Cory, she was going to spend an hour reading her Bible. The answers to reaching her son had to be there.

And maybe she'd also figure out how to deal with her escalating responses to Zac.

Chapter Six

"We're not going to leave you to eat alone, Brianna, so come on." Zac stemmed his irritation that she would rather eat alone than join him and Cory.

"But—"

"Kent can't make it tonight so it will be just the three of us." He saw her hesitation and pounced. "I know your dad is eating with your mom tonight. I met him on my way here, and he told me about the home's October Harvest Meal."

Brianna glanced from him to Cory.

"Come on, Mom. It'll be fun."

"If you're sure I won't be in the way." When they both agreed she wouldn't, Brianna finally accepted the invitation. "I'll have to catch a ride with you, though, Zac. My car is in the shop."

"Again," Cory muttered, rolling his eyes.

"It's not that bad." Brianna got in the front seat of Zac's car.

She wasn't sure about allowing Cory this privilege so soon after he'd messed up with his curfew, but she'd done her best to point out the seriousness of his bad choices and he'd seemed to pay attention. For this one evening she was not going to worry about Cory. She was going to relax and try to enjoy herself.

And it was fun. Especially because Cory dropped his macho act and allowed himself to be the kid he was.

"For a first-time griller, you did an awesome job, Cory." Zac savored his steak with appreciative eyes. "It's not everyone who can get a rare steak done perfectly. This one is."

"You did all the work. But thanks." Cory hid his burning cheeks by bending over his plate. But a minute later he glanced up to the plaque on the stone wall next to the barbecue. "What does that mean?" he asked.

Brianna read the words silently.

When He has tested me, I will come forth as gold.

"That's a very special verse my mom taught me years ago when I had to have a lot of surgeries." Zac smiled at him. "Sometimes I got really grumpy so one day my mother read me the story of Job. Do you know it?"

"Sort of." Cory leaned forward, his interest obvious.

"Well, to recap, Job had a lot of problems. He lost his family, his wealth and his health, but he didn't lose his faith, even when his friends tried to convince him he'd done something wrong." Zac pointed to the plaque. "That's what he said in the middle of all his trials. *When He has tested me, I will come forth as gold.* So I try to remember Job's faith when I get tested."

"Tested? You mean God tests you?" Cory's eyes widened.

"Of course. Faith in God means being strong." Zac shrugged. "That's what God's tests are all about. He needs us to learn how to keep doing the right thing, trusting in Him no matter what."

"Oh." Cory concentrated on his meal.

Brianna did, too, mulling over what Zac had said. Was

that the reason behind the hardship she struggled with? Was God testing her faith?

If so, she figured He must be disappointed. She hadn't had to endure years of surgeries as Zac had, though she had endured years of her mother's controlling. Still—she decided to think about it more later, when she was alone.

Once they'd finished their steaks, grilled potatoes and the Caesar salad Brianna had made, Zac surprised them with his grilled dessert—chocolate melted over sweet sliced peaches on a bed of crushed cookies.

"Wow!" Cory's pupils expanded. "I never knew guys could cook like this."

"Really?" Zac frowned at him. "Don't the guys you know eat?"

"Yes, but—" Cory glanced at Brianna.

"In my opinion, taking care of yourself is a basic skill every guy and girl ought to know," Zac said firmly. "If you can't even take care of yourself, how can you become an adult who has to be responsible for others?"

It was clear to Brianna that Cory had never considered this. After they'd cleared the dishes and stored them in the dishwasher, Cory wandered off to a spot in the yard where he sat down and stared at the plaque.

"Thank you for that," Brianna murmured. "It seems your words really hit home with him. Finally."

"Sometimes we have to hear things from a different person to get them through our thick heads." He offered her a mug of steaming tea and she took it, even though the evening retained much of its heat. "How do you think Your World is going to go over on Monday?" he asked.

"Zac, are you seriously worried about this?" Brianna could see by his furrowed brow that he was. "Why?"

"I have a lot riding on this project."

"You do? But you said you're staying behind the scenes."

As Brianna studied him she felt her body tense. He wasn't telling her something.

"I guess I've never really explained to you why I want this project to make such a difference here," he said, his voice grave.

"You *said* you wanted to challenge the students' apathy." She raised one eyebrow. "Was that a lie?"

"No, of course not. I do want that. Very much. But I have a second reason for wanting to see success in Hope's schools." Zac inhaled, then gazed directly at her. "I want to get into curriculum development, Brianna, at the state level."

"Ah." Understanding dawned. Her stomach took a nose-dive. "And to get that job you need a big success in Hope, success you want to achieve with the Your World project, so the folks in the state offices will see that your methods succeed, right? I get it."

Here she'd been entertaining thoughts of tenderness toward him, and it seemed Zac was using her. What a fool!

"Brianna—"

"Hope's failing schools are all part of your big plan. You were telling the truth when you said that's why you came back."

"Yes, but I wasn't trying to use you, Brianna," Zac rushed to reassure, dots of red coloring his prominent cheekbones. "I thought this would be good for your practice, too."

"Really? I think you thought giving Whispering Hope Clinic, me, the contract for school counseling was a way to make me so grateful I'd willingly help you with your big idea." She bit her lip to contain the words but they spilled out anyway. "It's the same old, same old, isn't it?"

"No," he objected, but it was a weak objection.

"Yes." Brianna set down her cup of tea, unable to swallow the very drink she'd been so happy he'd brewed moments before. "Back when we were to be married, you couldn't manage to be honest enough to tell me you'd accepted my mother's job. Now you can't be honest about your reasons for this project. I suppose you won't like hearing that Your World is actually causing a lot of problems at the clinic." Fury burned deep inside. Duped again. How dumb was she?

"What do you mean?" Zac stared at her.

"I mean that I've been working hard with several teens, trying to get them to see beyond their current circumstances to what the future could hold for them. But I'm fighting their parents every step of the way. They don't want their children to leave town any more than my mother wanted me to go way back when." She rose. "In fact, Eve Larsen's parents have been to see me twice, asking me to stop encouraging their daughter."

"Why would any parent object—"

"I can give you several reasons. They need their daughter in their business. Second, they think her goals are too lofty to succeed and, even if they weren't, they're worried about the expense. So you see, any benefit in my practice that I might have expected from Your World has already been negated by the Larsens bad-mouthing me all over town. I don't expect it to take long before other parents join their objections."

"I'm sorry. I didn't realize—"

"Exactly the point, Zac. You didn't realize. How could you? You were so focused on your own goal, you never gave a thought to what your scheme would mean to me or anyone else. But then it's always been all about you, hasn't it?" She grabbed her purse and sauntered toward the gate. "Stupid me. I thought you'd changed." She cut off the words, unwilling to admit she'd hoped things could change between them. "Cory, come on. We're leaving. Thanks for dinner. We'll walk home. I need the fresh air."

Though Cory gave her several speculative glances on the way home, he didn't ask any questions, choosing instead to disappear into his grandfather's studio in the garage where the two of them painted until bedtime. Brianna went into Cory's room to say good-night and praised his latest watercolor, a pretty picture of Zac's backyard.

"Good night, honey," she said as she hugged him, amazed as always that she was the mother of this amazing child. "Church tomorrow morning, don't forget."

"Yeah." Cory peered at her. "You're pretty steamed at Zac, aren't you?"

"Yes." There was no point in pretending otherwise.

"Why?"

"Because he didn't tell me the truth." Bitterness flowed inside. "I've known Zac for a long time. I thought we were friends."

"Sometimes people make mistakes, Mom." Cory's blue-eyed gaze held hers. "You always told me that God expects us to forgive and forget."

"Yes, I did. And I will. But I'm not there yet, son." She brushed his sandy brown hair off his forehead. "You're old enough to know that sometimes we have to work things through before we can find forgiveness in our heart."

"Is that what you're doing with Grandma? Finding forgiveness?"

"I'm trying, son. I'm trying. Have a good sleep."

Brianna wandered downstairs and found her father sipping a cup of cocoa.

"Warm night for that, isn't it?"

"Probably." He grinned. "But sometimes a cup of hot chocolate is exactly the medicine a body needs. Want some?"

"Yes." She accepted the steaming mug he handed her. "And, no, I don't want to talk about it," she hurried to say, seeing the speculation in his eyes.

"Okay." He led the way to the back patio where they both flopped onto comfortable lounge chairs around the pool.

Brianna sipped her chocolate as she struggled to figure out why she kept being disappointed in people. She needed to unload on someone so finally she blurted out, "Why doesn't God care about me, Dad?"

"Where did you get that idea?" he said, his voice calm in the dusky silence.

"I got that idea from all the bad things that keep happening to me." Again Brianna felt a surge of bitterness take hold.

"What makes you think you should be immune from bad things?" Brian Benson demanded. "Did someone promise you perfection?"

"No. But—" She frowned. Put that way she sounded childish. "So many things in my life have gone the opposite to what I expected," she admitted.

"Then maybe your expectations were wrong." He set down his cup and turned to face her. "Everyone's allowed to lapse into self-pity sometimes, Brianna, but if you stay there, you're heading for trouble."

Self-pity? She wanted to reject that, but maybe he was right.

"Honey, you have to trust the future to God. He has plans for you, though it might not seem like it now. You can't let the present problems obscure the future."

Brianna smiled. Wasn't that exactly what she'd been telling her clients? The old adage "Physician heal thyself," mocked her. She'd been pushing the kids she counseled, and their parents, to look for possibilities, and here she was doing what they did, letting current problems confound her.

"The thing is, it's called a 'faith walk' because you have to have faith to walk it," her father continued. "You can't know the answers ahead of time, no matter how much you want to. Believe me, I have my own whys that I'd like answered. But God doesn't owe me any answers." His voice grew serious. "Long ago I said He was Lord of my life. A servant doesn't ask the master why he has to do things. He just does them, trusting that the master has a good reason."

His words bit deep into Brianna's soul. That's what she'd been doing. Asking God to justify Himself to her.

"The Bible says the same thing a little differently. It says the clay doesn't look at the potter and say, 'Why did you make me into this kind of a pot? Change me. Make me that kind.'" He chuckled. "My dad told me that and it's stuck with me. Whenever I want to ask God why, I think of myself as a pot on the potter's wheel, one eye wide open, peering at the master potter and telling him how to make me. It makes me feel ridiculous every time."

"I can imagine." She watched while her father stretched, stood, picked up his cup and bent to brush his lips against her forehead. "Good night, Dad."

"Good night, honey." He walked to the back door, paused and then peered through the gloom at her. "Maybe it's time to start thinking about what God is trying to teach you."

Alone in the night, with the moon creeping into the starlit sky, Brianna felt ashamed of her attitude. Yes, it had been hard to raise Cory without his father, hard to learn after Craig's death that he'd known he would die soon and hadn't told her. It was hard to keep encouraging kids when the parents fought her so hard. It was more than hard to see her mother and be subjected to her verbal abuse every time.

Last Sunday's sermon echoed inside her head.

God never promised you a rose garden, but He said He'd be there to help you deal with the thorns.

Brianna resolved to change her thinking. She was still angry at Zac, and she'd have to work to get over that, but she'd also learned a lesson. Zac wasn't considering a future here in Hope. He had plans to move on, plans that made her silly daydreams of what might be futile.

Better to face that now before her heart got in any deeper.

"You are as close to God as you choose to be."

The minister's words hit Zac with the impact of a steel brick.

"Intimate friendship with God is a choice, not an accident," the pastor continued.

Wait a minute. Did that mean these feelings of uselessness that had plagued Zac for years—that was *his* fault? That God hadn't given up on him?

"If you want a more intimate connection with God, first of all you're going to have to learn to share your feelings with Him. All of them." The sermon seemed specially chosen for Zac. He couldn't have ignored the words if he wanted to.

"God doesn't expect His kids to be perfect. None of the great Biblical figures were perfect. If that was a requirement, none of us would attain His friendship. But God does expect your honesty, even if that involves messing up a million times. Even if it involves complaining and arguing with Him. Read the Psalms. David often accused God of unfairness, betrayal and even abandonment. He said, 'I pour out my complaints before Him and tell Him all my troubles. For I am overwhelmed.' David never pretended everything was okay between God and him."

Zac considered his attitude. He'd always believed he didn't possess the qualities God required in order to use someone, that he was a misfit and therefore unfit for God's work. After all he didn't have the same glib ability as his friends to talk to others about ordinary stuff, let alone about godly things. But that wasn't what the pastor was saying.

"If you read the Old Testament, you'll find God was very honest with His children. He got so fed up with Israel's dis-obedience in the desert He told Moses He would keep His promise regarding the Promised Land, but He refused to go one step farther. God was sick and tired of his kids!" The man joined the congregation's laughter. "I see some of you parents can relate. So don't worry, God can handle your honesty. He can handle your anger. But if you're going to be honest with God and others, you have to be honest with yourself. You have to open yourself up to others being honest with you."

And that was his stumbling block, Zac knew. He just couldn't let go of the fear that if he were honest, if he let someone see inside to all his cracks and weaknesses, they'd make fun of him. That's what terrified him, that people would see his insecurities and mock him as nothing but a teacher who couldn't even master his own issues. How could he help others?

Whatever was said next, Zac missed as he kept turning the issue over and over in his mind. Why was the deep in-timate kind of honesty so hard for him?

When the service ended, he saw Brianna greet Jaclyn and Kent, but though the couple waved, Brianna kept her head averted and soon left with Cory. She was still mad at him and he didn't blame her. He hadn't been honest with her about Your World just as he hadn't been honest all those years ago when he'd latched on to her mother's offer like a life preserver.

It was time—past time—to apologize to her.

Zac hurried out the door and searched the parking lot. He saw Brianna pulling away in her father's car. She didn't even glance his way though Zac saw Cory turn and wave.

"What's the rush, professor?" Kent stood behind him, peering down the street. "You missed Brianna."

"Thank you for that astute observation." Zac regretted the frustrated response as soon as he said it, but apparently Kent didn't take offense. He simply grinned. "I was hoping to apologize to her," Zac muttered.

"For what?" Kent's grin slid away. "You did something really stupid, didn't you?"

"Yes," Zac admitted freely.

"So make it right," his friend ordered before he loped back to his wife.

Yeah. Make it right. But how?

Honesty increases the level of intimacy. But if you're going to be honest with God and others, you have to open yourself up.

Open himself up—to Brianna? Could he do that again and risk leaving himself unprotected? Could he risk not doing it and losing Brianna's help?

Zac trudged the short distance to his home, struggling to dislodge the minister's words. But the words before the benediction hung in the back of his mind like a chant he couldn't ignore.

If you want to be close to God, then learn how to trust Him, no matter what He asks you to do.

Zac ate his lunch without tasting a thing as the inward battle raged.

Trust God?

That was the root of his problem.

Zac didn't trust anyone.

"These colors don't go together. If you'd stayed in the store and learned from me, you'd know that. I can't understand how you could be so stupid."

"Neither do I, Mom. Neither do I." A wealth of bitterness suffused her as Brianna gathered her array of quilt patches and stuffed them into her bag. She said a quick goodbye then left the room, tears overflowing the moment she stepped over the threshold. She felt rather than heard her father follow her and, for his sake, tried to regain her calm.

"Your mother loves you, Brianna. In spite of what you think."

"That was love?" She shook her head, her eyes clouded by tears.

"That was frustration." He wrapped an arm around her shoulder and squeezed.

"Dad, it's obvious that she hates me."

"No, she doesn't. She loves you very much. She just can't express it. She never learned how." He wiped away her tears. "Try to imagine her world. She wakes up and she's here, alone. She doesn't always remember why she's here or where we are. She doesn't know what's going to happen to her. She can't get the words she needs to communicate, to express what she wants. Everything has changed and she's confused and angry and hurt and scared. And, yes, she takes it out on you. But that doesn't mean she doesn't love you."

"Ha! You heard what she said. Being called *stupid* is a strange form of love." Brianna gulped. "I've made quilts for years, and sold many of them to people who claimed I have a knack for blending colors and textures. I paid for my schooling that way. But my own mother can't see any potential in my work. What kind of love is that?"

"She does love you," her dad insisted.

Brianna sniffled her disbelief. She pressed away from him, her eyelashes damp and stuck together.

"I stayed away all these years because she wanted her disappointing daughter out of her life, so I wouldn't ruin her success. I came back because you said she wanted me here, but that's not true. She doesn't want me here. I'm still the bad daughter who wouldn't become part of her business." Her lips tightened. "I've had it, Dad. I'm sick of being put down so she'll feel better. It's better if I don't come here anymore. Less upsetting for both of us."

"No." Mr. Benson clasped his daughter's shoulders and forced her to look at him. "Your mother does not hate you, Brianna. She never has."

"I don't believe you." Brianna saw Zac coming toward them from down the hall. She blew her nose and thrust back her shoulders. "And I don't want to talk about this anymore."

"I do, but we'll have to discuss it later. I'm going back in to make sure Anita's settled. I'll see you at home." He hurried into the room just as his wife called for him.

"I need to talk to you, Brianna." Zac stood in front of her, blocking her exit.

"Isn't it amazing that even after all those years of her running him ragged, Dad still worships the ground my mother walks on?" Brianna muttered as she glared at him.

"I don't know." He frowned. "Did you hear me?"

"I don't want to talk to you or anyone right now, Zac." She walked around him, down the hall and out into the parking lot. "I just want to get out of here."

"I'll take you for a ride."

"I'd rather be alone." She strode away, furious that he thought he could just waltz back into her life after using her to get his big master plan under way.

"I'm not going away and you won't shake me until I say what I came to say." Though she ignored him, he kept pace easily, modulating his steps to hers.

The afternoon was warm and it wasn't long before Brianna began to perspire. It was clear that Zac wasn't going to be brushed off so easily. Tired, cranky and fed up with her life, she jerked to a halt and wheeled around to face him.

"What do you want?" she demanded. "Today's my day off. I'm not available to give you counseling about your new goal. Or anything else. I need to figure out how I'm going to get to Las Cruces and pick up Cory's birthday present before his party tomorrow. So whatever you need, you'll have to handle it yourself."

"I could take you."

"No, thanks." She glared at him. No way did she want to spend the afternoon tied in knots because of Zac Ender.

"Please, Brianna. Just listen." He gazed at her, his dark eyes serious. "I'm sorry. I mean that sincerely. I apologize for not telling you what I was planning. At first I didn't even think about it mattering to you, and then later—"

"Later I stupidly fell in with your plan, like the idiot I am, and you decided not to give me the consideration of telling me the reason you sucked me into the whole thing. Is that what you're saying, Zac?" She loaded the words with as much scorn as she could, still stinging from her mother's rejection.

"Not exactly what I meant." Zac frowned, hesitated, but after a moment, nodded. "But if that works for you, then, yes, that's what I'm saying."

"Some apology." Brianna hissed a sigh from between her teeth, glaring at him in utter frustration. "Just like before. When are you going to figure out that all you have to do is be honest, Zac? I would have helped you anyway because I care about helping the kids in this town. What would it have cost you to tell me the truth?"

"A lot." He shrugged. "I don't open up to people easily. You know that. You know that I'm a klutz at human relationships."

"That's your favorite song, isn't it? I can't help it. That's the way God made me." She moved so her face was inches from his and glared into his eyes. "It's baloney, and you know it. You aren't a klutz when you forget about your silly preconceptions. It's when you get the focus off of others and on to yourself that you mess up."

Chapter Seven

Zac flinched, decimated by her diagnosis of his problem. But more than that, with that simple touch on his arm, she'd reached past his self-imposed barriers to reignite that part of him that was not immune to her.

He was tired of this age-old reaction to Brianna, the fizzling spear of tenderness that flamed whenever he looked at her, then shot straight to his gut, doubling his nervousness in spite of his determination to remain unflappable. He was tired of his inability to erase the blaze of feeling he'd had ten years ago. Mostly he was tired of always trying to measure up and feeling like he constantly fell short.

He spared a moment to wonder if God was fed up with him.

Zac inhaled and forced out the words he should have said weeks ago. "I don't want us to be at loggerheads, Brianna. We have to work together. I screwed up. I didn't tell you my plans when I asked for your help and I should have. I'm sorry and I apologize."

There. He'd said it. There was nothing else to say. He turned and walked toward his car.

"That's it?" She grabbed his arm and drew him to a halt. "That's all you have to say?"

"What more do you want?" Anger that she kept pushing him bubbled inside. "I messed up. Again. Is that what you wanted to hear?"

"No. I'd like to hear why you're doing Your World." Her beautiful eyes impaled him. "What's the big draw working at state level?"

Zac studied her, searching for the best way to explain because he knew she wouldn't let it go. "Curriculum, which I've always wanted to be involved in."

"I get that. But that's not all of it," she challenged. "Be honest with me, Zac."

"Curriculum is primarily office work. Developmental."

"Uh-huh." Brianna's sandal-clad feet were planted, her stance combative.

"In curriculum I won't have to do any public presentations," he finally blurted out.

"But—you've always been so great with kids. You used to live to get in the classroom and make education come alive. You're willing to give that up?" The green of her eyes darkened to a forest tone. Her mouth formed an *O*. "You will, won't you? To avoid public speaking."

"Yes," he agreed, wondering if he looked as small as he now felt.

"But you're not required to do a lot of speaking now."

"Assembly tomorrow," he reminded her, dread dogging his spirit. "The parents will be there."

"So what? They're mostly people we went to school with."

"Exactly." He could imagine what they'd think when nerdy Zac Ender stuttered his way through an explanation of Your World.

"Most parents' concern is that their kids do well. They're not going to be focused on you as much as the program."

Brianna craned her neck forward, scrutinizing his face. "You're really that bothered?"

"Yes," Zac assured her, embarrassed by the admission. "If you remember, I was never that good at presentations, and trust me, I have not improved with age."

"Yes, but—" She spluttered, obviously at a loss. "But I've seen you with the kids. You're not nervous when you're with them."

"Sometimes I am, but it's easier to hide it with kids. Not so easy with adults. Especially ones who knew me in the good old days." He shrugged. She wanted honesty? Okay, let's see how she handled him baring his soul. "I freeze up, Brianna. I get tongue-tied and I don't make sense, even to myself. Who wants to listen to that?"

"But you can't just opt out. Not now." She gave him a speculative glance. "Your World is *your* project. You have to be involved. Publicly involved," she emphasized.

"I will be." Humiliated and embarrassed, Zac wanted this conversation to end. "Forget my problems. What I wanted to do today was apologize for not telling you my plans. Now that I've done that, I'll go and let you enjoy your afternoon."

He'd almost made it to his car when she spoke again.

"Is the offer of a ride to Las Cruces still on?"

"Sure." He turned, studied her face, wondering if she would accept his help because she felt sorry for him.

"My car is still in the shop, and I'd really like to pick up Cory's birthday gift." She must have read something on his face because after a moment Brianna shook her head. "Never mind. I'll think of something else."

"I'll take you. I can pick up a book on South America that's waiting for me." Zac realized he welcomed the afternoon away from town. And with Brianna? "Do you have to be home in time to make dinner tonight?"

"Dad will eat with Mom, and Cory's on that youth-group riding outing. They're having a fire and picnic after so he won't be home till eight or so." She wore a funny look that told him she expected he'd change his mind. "Why?"

"Just thinking. Let's go."

But Brianna didn't move. "Are you sure you want to do this?"

"Yes." Though Zac expected some leftover tension to tinge their afternoon, once they were on the highway Brianna told him she accepted his apology.

"I understand this curriculum job is a big deal to you and that you don't want anything to ruin it," she mused, peering out the windshield at the golden swells of the hills. "So I'll forgive you this time. But, Zac, you have to be honest with me. I refuse to work with you on Your World anymore unless you tell me the truth."

"Okay." He glanced from the road to her, knowing by her tone that there was something else Brianna wanted to say. "And?"

"I don't believe your issues with public speaking are something you can't overcome."

"Overcome how?" Not that Zac intended to change his mind about moving to Santa Fe for curriculum work, but he wanted to hear Brianna's thoughts on defeating the bugaboo that had haunted him for years.

"You won't like what I'm about to say," she warned with a sideways glance at him.

"I'll handle it," he told her in a dry tone.

"Okay." She studied him for a moment. "In my experience, issues like yours stem from an overfocus on yourself."

"Hey!" Zac twisted his head to frown at her.

"I warned you that you wouldn't like it. Now let me finish." Brianna waited for his nod before continuing. "The most effective public speakers, the ones we love to listen to, aren't thinking about themselves when they speak. What they're concentrating on is their audience, on getting their message across. They've got something to say and they're focused on making a point, not on whether their audience will notice if they stumble or make a mistake or pause too long. It's the message, not the messenger. But because they are so good at getting that message to us, we say they are good public speakers."

"You're saying I'm getting in the way of what I want to say." His lips pinched together. The truth hurt.

"Yes, but it's more than that." Brianna looked at him, visibly debating her next words.

"I won't melt from criticism. Go on," he told her.

"If you could forget about what you feel like and focus on what your listeners feel like, on how they're accepting what you have to tell them, you'd forget to be so self-conscious."

"You make me sound selfish." He glanced at Brianna and knew that was exactly what she meant.

"Because I think it is selfish to worry more about your-self than the message." She opened her handbag, a turquoise satchel she usually looped over one shoulder.

That was the thing about Brianna—she knew how to make a point. She could carry off a vibrant color like tur-quoise because she herself was so dynamic. Little things like speaking to a crowd of people didn't affect her. Obliv-ious to his scrutiny, she pulled out a small notepad and began writing on it.

"In the presentation tomorrow, for instance, you have to make sure the students realize that no idea they have is unworthy of writing on the board. You need to ensure that they and their dreams are valued. That has to be your pri-mary focus."

"I *was* having a relaxed afternoon," Zac grumbled. "Now I'm getting all uptight about tomorrow and that speech."

"But that's the thing—you're not giving a speech. You are simply explaining how a new program is going to work." Brianna shook her dark head at him, her eyes twinkling. "It's not a lecture, nor do you have to defend anything. You're just explaining and you've done that with students for years. Haven't you?"

"Yes." But admitting that fact did nothing to untie the knot in his midsection. So he turned the focus on her. "What did you think of the sermon today?"

Brianna was quiet for so long Zac was ready to change the subject.

"What the pastor said about friendship with God, that was interesting." She averted her head and stared out the side window. "That God wants—even welcomes—frank honesty from us—I guess I've never thought that way. He said genuine friendship is built on disclosure. God wanting to be friends is a different perspective for me."

"Because you don't like to think of God as a friend?" Zac found himself curious about the wan look filling her expressive eyes.

"It's not that. I guess I've never thought that it was perfectly okay to blurt out what you really feel. To anyone."

"That's why you never told me about the problems between you and your mom." Zac watched her shift and knew his guess was on target. "Because you had to hide your feelings?"

"Because it was embarrassing. I didn't want my friends to hear her rant." She frowned. "I was raised that talk to God should be reverent. To think that it's okay to tell Him you feel cheated or disappointed in Him, that's odd to me."

"Do you feel cheated and disappointed?" Zac asked quietly.

"Yes." Brianna looked at him steadily. "Yes, I do."

"Why?" Zac recalled the minister's words that a block to true friendship was often hidden anger or resentment.

"I don't understand why He doesn't answer prayers, why He allows certain things. If I were God I would never let children die from starvation," she said, her voice hard. "I wouldn't let people who cause misery and suffering go scot-free and I wouldn't make the innocent suffer. How can I build a friendship with God when He allows this?"

Zac recalled the years after she'd jilted him and the months after that he'd wasted asking why. He'd drifted from God in the intervening years, but he'd finally learned to face himself and all his faults. The lesson had stuck. He was determined to share it now. Maybe, for once, he could be the one to help her.

"Anger, frustration, bitterness—those kind of feelings are natural," he assured her. "You, as a psychologist, must know that giving voice to them and releasing them is the first step toward healing. You were talking earlier about honesty. Isn't it the ultimate honesty to tell God exactly how you feel?"

"I suppose. But what good does it do?" she demanded. "It changes nothing."

"Not if you leave it at that." Zac shifted in his seat, slightly uncomfortable with how personal this conversation was becoming. He wasn't the kind of Christian that God used to help other people, but he couldn't leave Brianna floundering in her anger.

"So?" She frowned at him, waiting.

"The thing is, you have to not only realize but also accept that God acts in your best interest, always, even when it's painful and you don't understand. The pastor said worship is about holding back nothing of what you feel. If God didn't want to hear what we really thought, He wouldn't have allowed Psalms to be in the Bible. It sounded like he was saying that expressing doubt is the first step to building a rapport with God."

The tip of Brianna's pert nose scrunched up as if she thought he was full of hot air.

"It's a process, and I'm no expert," Zac told her. "But He said that every time you trust God's wisdom and do as He asks in spite of your misgivings or lack of understanding, you make the relationship more real. So I guess it boils down to whether we are willing to trust Him or not." Trust again. Something sadly lacking in his own life.

"Trust?"

"Yeah. Something I find hard to do." He dredged his brain for the applications he'd studied ten years ago and still struggled to implement. "If we're truly followers of Christ, we follow Him. Meaning we do as He asks. But not because we're afraid of Him, or from guilt or fear of punishment, but because we love Him. And because we love, therefore we trust that He knows what's best for us—in spite of our perceptions of the current state."

Brianna studied him through narrowed eyes.

"What?" Zac felt his cheeks burn at the intense scrutiny. "Why are you looking at me like that?"

"Did you just hear yourself?" she said, a smile tipping her mouth at one corner. "You didn't stutter or stammer or mess up your message. You got it out with clarity and conviction."

"I wasn't speaking in public."

"What difference does that make? You were trying to get something across and you did it because you weren't focused on yourself or how you felt, but on what you wanted me to understand." She leaned forward, her face serious. "If you could just see yourself with the kids, Zac, you'd realize that you do the same thing with them. That's why you're such a great teacher."

"Thanks, but I'm nothing special."

"I give up," Brianna said in frustration. "If you won't see the gift you have, I can't make you."

As he took the exit ramp that led to the mall they'd decided to visit, Zac considered Brianna's words. The gift he had? That was Brianna the nurturer. But all the same, on the drive home he'd treat her to dinner and then ask her help with what he planned to say tomorrow. Maybe she could keep him from totally embarrassing himself in front of the entire school.

And after that he was going to do some serious thinking about his spiritual relationship.

"I've got several things to pick up." Brianna stood inside the mall doors, shifting uncomfortably under Zac's scrutiny. "Shall we meet in a couple of hours?"

They agreed on a time and a place then Brianna set off to collect the gifts she'd chosen for Cory. Fortunately the store had a clearance on the game system she'd planned to purchase, which allowed her to add a couple of the games that Cory was crazy about. She'd save those for Christmas gifts.

Since Brianna completed her shopping well before the appointed time, she strolled through a quilt store, pretending to envision a new project. But in fact she couldn't dislodge the picture of Zac's face when he'd told her his thoughts on faith. She'd never seen such openness from him before. The strength of his convictions seemed so clear.

Yet he still feared public speaking.

Was part of that her fault? Because she'd left so quickly the morning of the wedding, she hadn't considered what Zac would have to endure. The first thing she'd ever learned about Zac Ender was how much he hated being the focus of anything. She'd attributed that to the years he'd been a patient, with his mother and medical team constantly watching his every move. So to endure a year of gossip and ridicule while he taught must have been desperately difficult.

She owed him an apology. She'd been so immersed in her own pain that day, she hadn't realized how running away from the wedding would affect him.

Brianna shuddered at the thought of harking back to the past again. Yes, she still resented Zac's betrayal of their dreams, their future. It festered like a sore that had never really healed. How could he have given them up so easily? Why hadn't God done something to stop it?

But though she'd asked many times, God still gave no explanation.

Brianna glanced at the clock in the window of a bookstore. Fifteen minutes until she joined Zac. Time enough to go in and see if there was something that could help her find answers to the soul-deep questions that plagued her. She added a devotional book she'd heard Cory mention the youth group using to his birthday gifts, but saw nothing for herself.

"Please help me understand, God," she begged under her breath in a desperate plea as she wandered between the shelves. Nothing. Too embarrassed to ask for help she decided to check out.

"Is that everything for you?" the clerk asked.

"Yes, thanks." Brianna set her items on the counter, wishing that just this once God would have answered.

"I hope you found what you needed," the clerk said as she bagged the items. "I didn't mean to ignore you. It's just that we've got some new stock and I'm trying to get everything shelved before my boss comes in tomorrow morning."

"No problem." Brianna hurried away, not wanting to keep Zac waiting. Maybe on the way home she could find an opportunity to apologize to him. Maybe if she did, she'd finally learn why he'd given up on their dreams.

"You look like your mission was successful." Zac took her packages. "Do you need more time? I could put these in the car."

"No, thanks. I'm finished." She glanced around. "I could use a coffee, though."

"How about if we do the drive-through thing and take it to the park. It's a gorgeous day." Zac waited for her nod then walked with her to the car. "Hey, we could head out to see the hot-air balloons." He pointed to a poster stuck to a light standard. "Today's the last day of the festival."

Brianna drew on the hazy memory of an afternoon spent with Zac, watching the beauty of the multicolored balloons as he explained how the air filling them lifted the colorful balls with baskets attached high over the white gypsum dunes. Peaceful, relaxing. It was just the thing she needed on this Sunday afternoon.

"I haven't been out there in years," she admitted. That long-ago Saturday had been one of a very few her mother had allowed her to take off from work at the store. She and Zac had left home early, spread a blanket on the hills and huddled together in the cool air to wait for that breathless moment of lift-off when the balloons became airborne.

"Me, neither. Let's go." Zac hummed a tune as he loaded both their parcels in the back of his car.

The crystal clarity of the atmosphere and the heat of the autumn sun offered the perfect opportunity to admire miles of the desert sky. They arrived and found their favorite spot. Brianna blinked at the quilt Zac dragged out of his car.

"You're still using this old thing?" she asked, fingering the threadbare corners she'd so painstakingly stitched for his Christmas gift in their senior year of college.

"Quality never grows old," he said with a wink and chuckled at her droll look.

His laughter brought back so many memories of days

they'd laughed and giggled, making the hours of studying so much fun. She'd forgotten the joy of those times, or maybe she'd let it get tarnished by anger and frustration. Now Brianna released that and resolved to enjoy the moment.

As they sat on the hillside, she couldn't stop taking little peeks at Zac as he sipped his coffee and watched balloons dot the horizon in front of them.

"Tell me." Zac pointed to the bold colors laid out in a panorama before them. "Did you ever see anything like that in Chicago?"

"No." She kept her head averted. "But Chicago had other assets."

"One of them being your husband, I suppose." His voice dropped. "What was he like?"

Zac sounded so—intense. Brianna risked a quick look at him, found him staring at her with those dark riveting eyes. His curiosity was probably as natural as hers was when she thought about all the years they'd been apart. It couldn't hurt to tell him. In fact, the words came easily. Of all the betrayals, it was Craig's that she found easiest to forgive.

"Craig was my friend, a real friend when I needed one most."

"How did you meet?"

"Actually I met him and Cory on the train in Las Cruces the day I left home. Craig wasn't feeling well and poor Cory was teething. While Craig rested, I kept Cory entertained. He was such a cute baby. I felt so sad that his mom had died in childbirth. He never knew her." Which was only part of the reason Brianna now felt such responsibility to ensure Cory got the love and support he needed. With Craig gone, there was only her.

"Go on." A tinge of diffidence underlay Zac's voice.

"Not much else to tell, really." Brianna remembered the train trip as if it were yesterday. "As we traveled, we talked.

Craig told me about a job in a friend's office, another doctor. He helped me get it. He also helped me find a place to live once we arrived in Chicago. As thanks, I babysat for him. We got to know each other. A few months later I agreed to marry him."

"Why?" Zac's mouth was tight.

"Craig needed someone to help him with Cory." She shook her head, a smile of regret clouding her memories. "I didn't know at the time, but Craig was terminally ill with cancer. His treatment left him incapable of caring for Cory. We weren't in love or anything. I agreed to marry him so I could look after Cory full time. He died a few months after we were married."

"I'm glad for Cory." Zac's voice emerged low and intense. "If not for you, who knows what would have happened to him. He's very lucky you were willing to give up your life for him."

"It wasn't exactly like that," she said, brushing off his compliment. But in actual fact, it had been for the first while. "Of course, at first it was difficult. Cory had a tough time teething. There were a lot of late nights."

"It must have been hard for you to be widowed with an infant." Zac touched her arm, his brown eyes soft with empathy. "Why didn't you come home? Surely your parents could have helped."

"You'd think so, wouldn't you?" Instantly Brianna's soft memories hardened into a ball of resentment. She couldn't speak for a moment, so great was her fury.

"What happened, Brianna?" Zac's soft pleading was her undoing.

"Does it matter?" Her joy in the afternoon dissolved, Brianna jumped to her feet. "Can we go now? It's been nice, but I don't want to be too late getting home. I don't want Cory to go out with his friends again tonight."

Zac rose without comment and folded the old quilt. He walked with her to his car and unlocked it. But before she could get inside, he laid his hand on her arm, his fingers curling against her skin, leaving a trail of heat.

Brianna stared at him, waiting for his condemnation.

"I'm sorry, Brianna. Really sorry. If I'd known you needed help, I'd have been there." He studied her for several moments, and then with a last touch, he opened the car door.

She couldn't get over his words, or the way he'd said them. Tender. Comforting. Not at all condemning. And that's when she knew it was time.

"Zac." She turned to face him when they were back on the highway. "I've waited too long to say this, and you probably don't care anyway, but I'm really sorry I left the way I did. I've been so wrapped up in my own side of things all these years, that I never really thought about what it must have been like for you. And I should have. Hope isn't kind to its citizens sometimes."

As she spoke, she saw a mask fall over his features, hardening them. His voice grated when he turned to glance at her.

"Why did you leave like that?" he asked. "You owed me better than that."

"Yes, I did." She admitted it freely. "I should have—"

"No." He held up a hand to stop her. "You know what? Don't say anymore. It doesn't matter now anyway. The past is over and as it turned out, it was the best thing for everybody." The accelerator inched up before he lifted his foot and visibly let go of the strain that had contorted his mouth into a tight line. "Let's just forget it."

The words killed her apology quicker than anything else could have. Zac thought it was best that she'd left? Then he certainly couldn't have any feelings for her now. Maybe he hadn't then, either. He made it sound as if their love had never been anything more than two kids with a crush on each other and yet to her it had been so much more. Brianna had never loved anyone as she'd loved him.

When Zac asked her if she wanted to listen to music, she agreed, glad he chose fast upbeat music that quashed the intimacy of the moment.

They stopped for an early dinner at a small roadside restaurant. Seated across from him on the patio, Brianna realized they had been here once before, during their Christmas break. They'd been so happy then, newly engaged, planning their marriage and eager to escape everyone to share some alone time.

Her old engagement ring lay under her shirt, pressing against her collar bone. Its presence reminded her of the way Zac had looked at her that night—adoringly. Now nothing on his chiseled face bore anything remotely resembling tenderness. Apparently no fond recollections of their shared past in this place bothered him or he wouldn't have chosen it. But Brianna was deluged by a ton of memories—of the big barrel cactus beside her that had been draped in tiny Christmas lights and the way Zac had nudged her behind it to share a quick kiss under a sprig of mistletoe.

For a moment utter loss overwhelmed her. Why had she let their love go so easily? Why hadn't she fought for him?

"So how is Cory doing?"

Zac's words snapped Brianna out of her daydream. "Pardon?"

"I take it those friends of his haven't disappeared."

"No, and I'm getting more worried every time he goes off with them." She played with her water glass while wondering how much to confess. "Lately I've begun wondering if they were the source of the drugs. Cory won't say who gave him that drink, but the way they act—" She shook her head. "Maybe I'm just too suspicious."

"Maybe you're right to be concerned."

Brianna hoped Zac would remember his promise to engage Cory, but when he said nothing, she decided to leave it for tonight. She suspected he'd become fixated on giving his upcoming speech.

During the ride home they talked of inconsequential things. Brianna was glad when they finally pulled into her driveway.

"Thanks very much for taking me to Las Cruces, Zac," she said as he trailed behind her into the house. "I appreciate it. And dinner. And the balloons."

"No problem." He stood there, as if waiting.

"Would you like to come in for a cup of coffee?" she asked, wondering if there was something else he wanted to say.

But he shook his head.

"Thanks, but I need to get home. I missed my run yesterday so I'll catch up tonight." His eyes searched hers until he finally looked away.

"Okay. Well, thanks again." Brianna waited, but it seemed Zac wasn't finished.

He scanned the room, and then finally, when she was about to speak, asked, "You will be there tomorrow, for assembly. Won't you?"

"Sure. If you want me to." She grabbed her bag and pulled out her day planner. "I have a meeting with Eve Larsen's parents but I think I can still make it."

"More complaints?" Zac asked, one eyebrow tilted.

"Eve's talking of becoming a doctor," Brianna confided. "She's asked Jaclyn all kinds of questions, even shadowed her on the job for a couple of hours to get a better idea of what is involved. With a little emphasis on study, I don't see why she couldn't attain that goal."

"But her parents don't agree?" Zac asked, frowning.

"Her father wants her to stay here so she can continue to work in their restaurant. Help is expensive." Eve's situation was so similar to Brianna's as a teen that she frequently had to remind herself not to make comparisons. "They'll ask me to try to dissuade her or at least lead her in a different direction. I'll lay out a few of the issues she'll face, of course, but that girl has a dream. Why shouldn't she at least try to pursue it?"

"I understand the parents' concern, though. They must be really strapped right now." Zac frowned. "Things are a little better in town since the mine opened, but how can they make up for all the years and lost business while Hope was in a decline?"

"I hope you're not going to tell me to kill Eve's dream," Brianna said. She heard the sour tone in her voice and tried to modulate it. "She wants out of Hope, Zac. She realizes she made a mistake, that drugs aren't the way to go. She's pouring herself into a new dream. She wants to show her parents that she's not a little girl anymore. But if they won't accept her goal, I don't know that I can help her, or them, anymore."

"I see." Zac looked at her for several moments. "Well, if they come to me, you know I'll support you. I'll even do some checking to see what funding there might be for someone in her situation. My whole focus is to get students to dream bigger. Clearly that's what you have Eve doing. It's what we need to get all the students to do."

"I believe Your World will be the first step for a lot of them," Brianna agreed. "All you have to do tomorrow is get the parents to see that."

"No pressure. Thanks," Zac said in a dry mocking tone. He lifted a hand and left.

Brianna watched him drive away, then lugged her packages upstairs to her room. She tucked Cory's gifts in her closet, noting that she'd inadvertently acquired Zac's book with her own packages. She set it aside to return to him. So much for avoiding him.

Another surprise waited. When Brianna removed Cory's book from the plastic bookstore bag, she found another much smaller booklet underneath it. She remembered there had been a stack of this title on the counter, but she hadn't intended to purchase one. Still, according to the receipt she had bought this tiny book.

She glanced at the title. *Knowing God.* Was that really possible?

She had about a half hour before Cory or her dad would return so Brianna sat down on her bed and began reading. The first words hit her straight between the eyes.

Pain is God's way of rousing us from spiritual lethargy. Problems aren't always punishment, sometimes they are wake-up calls from a God who is mad about you, not at you. He's trying to get you back into fellowship with Him. Read Jeremiah 29:13.

Intrigued, Brianna grabbed her Bible and read the passage. Basically it said that when she was ready to get really serious about knowing God, He wouldn't disappoint. Well, she was serious about it now. But what did it mean for her life? Her mother, Cory, work issues, even her difficulties with Zac—all of that was because God was trying to get her attention?

He had it!

Ready to read on, Brianna paused, recalling her desperate prayer for help in the bookstore. A fizzle of excitement started in her stomach and worked its way up to her brain.

God had answered her prayer! He'd led her to this book. Perhaps this little book could help her discern the Bible for her situation. A seed of hope sent out a shoot of hope.

Maybe if she studied hard enough, dug hard enough, God would finally show her why her life was in such turmoil.

And maybe then her brain would finally accept that Zac could never be a part of her life again.

Chapter Eight

"L-Ladies and gentlemen, teachers and students." Zac glanced around the room, searching for Brianna's face, needing the confidence her gorgeous eyes would impart.

She wasn't here. In a flash the same nemesis of fear that had dragged at him for most of his life, clawed its way to his throat, blocking it.

"I—ah, that is—"

Desperately, Zac scanned the crowd again. But Brianna was not present. Every eye in the room was on him, waiting. He had to continue.

Zac licked his lips, breathed a prayer and dove in to explain Your World. By the time fifteen minutes had lapsed, he knew his presentation was an unmitigated disaster, and so did everyone in the room. But he was determined to make sure the students understood the concept.

"Are there any questions?" he asked. To his surprise, Cory's hand went up. "Yes, Cory."

"Can we write anything on the board?"

"Within bounds." Zac peered at the young man, wondering why he'd asked the question. He listed the absolute no-nos again then went on to encourage all the students to take an active part. The ho-hum response he got was not encouraging, but there was little else he could say. No one seemed interested in Your World now, and for some reason that made Zac furious at Brianna. She'd promised to show. Where was she?

As the students left the room, he gathered his notes and left the platform. Brianna met him outside the door.

"Sorry I'm late," she puffed, obviously short of breath. Her hair was disheveled, too, the usual wispy curls out of place. "How did it go?"

"Even worse than I expected, which means it was bad." He pursed his lips, edged past her and walked out of the school, annoyed that she tagged along beside him.

"I'm sure it wasn't as terrible as you think, Zac."

"Really?" His temper flaring, he threw his suit jacket and his notes in the backseat of his car, then whirled around to face her. "Do you ever keep your promises and show up when you're supposed to?"

"That's not fair!" Brianna's green eyes widened with shock. She took a step back, her gaze narrowing. "I was working," she reminded him. "Doing my job."

"I guess that's as good an excuse as any." He yanked open the driver's door.

"Hey! What exactly did you expect me to do?" she demanded, grabbing his arm so he couldn't escape.

"Help me." The plea sputtered out on its own accord, and Zac felt a fool for having uttered it. All he wanted to do was leave, but Brianna's wounded stare forced him to explain. "You could have answered questions, clarified points—something."

"But you never told me you wanted me to do that," she protested. "You said I should drop by. Or at least that was my impression." Her forehead wrinkled. "I can't remember exactly what you said, but you knew I had a parent conference this morning, because I told you."

"You also said you'd be here." Zac clamped his lips together. What was the point of repeating that? She hadn't been bothered to make the effort. He was stupid to have thought she would care about his presentation enough to attend. "Look, I messed up and I'm in a foul mood, Brianna. I'm sorry. It's not your fault and I don't mean to take it out on you, it's just that I had such high expectations for this whole thing and now—" He left it hanging. His phone bleeped. He looked at it. "I have to go. I have to do a teacher evaluation this afternoon."

"But—"

Zac pretended he didn't hear as he got in the car and drove away.

His miserable presentation had only proven what he'd always believed—God had a tough time using someone like him to make a difference.

"Cory, do you think you could run that over to Zac?" Brianna pointed to the purple bag on the counter, then checked on the pan of chicken breasts browning in the oven.

Her father would be here with her mother shortly. There wasn't much time to make everything perfect, and it needed to be or her mother would be sure to point out her failure.

"Aw, Mom!" Cory glared at her. "The guys are coming soon for my birthday."

"I'll make sure they don't run away until you get back," she teased. "Take your bike. It won't take you long."

"What is this, anyway?" he asked, jiggling the bag.

"A book Zac special ordered. I took it with my packages by mistake yesterday." She raised her eyebrows at him. "Would you mind hurrying? I want you to be here when Grandma and Grandpa arrive."

"You didn't tell me Grandma was coming." He glared at her.

"I didn't know. Grandpa decided this afternoon to bring her." Brianna endured his angry look for a moment before asking, "Cory?"

"Yeah?"

"Were you at Mr. Ender's presentation this morning?"

"Yeah." His voice was hesitant.

"It was bad?" she asked, watching his face.

"Like really bad. I asked a question just so he could explain some more, but it didn't do much good."

Cory hunched his shoulders as he looked at her. "What's his issue anyway?"

"Zac doesn't like being in the spotlight. Never has as long as I've known him."

"You went to high school together, right?" Cory glared at her. "Kent told me that you and your friends were close. You've helped people with problems like Mr. Ender's before. So why don't you help him?"

"I'd like to, Cory. But Zac's had this problem for a long time. It's not going to disappear easily. It's kind of like you when you were afraid of heights. It took a while for you to realize you didn't need to be afraid. Zac is going to have to figure it out his own way." She felt a little strange about saying that but it was true. She could not give Zac what he needed. "So no one really got what Your World is all about?"

"The principal made an announcement after lunch and talked about it a lot. He said he wanted to clear up questions, but I think it was to cover for Mr. Ender. Anyway, I think everybody understood." He fiddled with the bag. "How long till Grandma comes?" Cory had formed a special bond with his grandmother, one which Brianna constantly worried over. She didn't want her son to catch her mother's negative attitude toward her.

"She should be here soon. Better get going," she urged.

"I'll be right back." Cory raced out the door. A second later she saw him speeding down the driveway.

Brianna watched him with a lump in her throat.

"I know you're there, God. Please make this a happy day for Cory. This one time, don't let Mom spoil it."

Ten minutes later her parents arrived at the same time as Cory's pals. Conversation was awkward, especially after Brianna's mother chided the boys about their manners. Brianna tried to cover, but all the same she heaved a sigh of relief when she saw Cory ride up. She almost choked when Zac appeared behind him.

"Mom!" Cory burst through the door. "I invited Zac to my birthday dinner." He returned Brianna's glare with a grin. "He told me to call him that. Anyway, he said he was going to eat leftovers so I invited him." Cory's facial expression made it clear that he thought leftovers were a fate worse than death.

"Great. Welcome, Zac," Brianna said cheerfully, inwardly chagrined. "Well, dinner's ready so let's eat." Her new plan to avoid Zac as much as possible was going up in smoke, especially after her father insisted Zac sit next to Brianna.

Her father said grace, then turned to his wife. "Isn't this a wonderful meal for our grandson's birthday?"

"I hope you enjoy it," Brianna said before her mother could denigrate her work. "There's plenty for everyone. Help yourselves."

Despite attempts to circumvent her mother's criticisms, the meal progressed with negative remarks about everything Brianna had worked so hard to create, followed by anecdotes about how her mother preferred to serve the item. Cory's friends snickered a couple of times while Zac interrupted to offer his compliments on the food.

Cory seemed oblivious to his grandmother's complaints,

his eyes fixed adoringly on her. From time to time Brianna's mother reached out to brush his hair off his forehead or pat his shoulder and he grasped her hand, the bond between them obvious. Brianna felt like an outsider.

Brianna had always baked and decorated her son's cake herself, rejecting the perfection of a bakery cake, as her mother had always done, for homemade love. This birthday was no exception. She carried the painstakingly decorated chocolate layers to the table with candles blazing, leading everyone in the birthday song. She loved this child so much.

"Mom makes the best birthday cakes, Grandma. Wait till you taste it. It's triple chocolate." Cory blew out the candles. "I'll cut you a piece."

"No, thank you, dear. I simply can't tolerate sickly sweet things. But Brianna knows that. I'm sure she's prepared something else for me."

In fact Brianna hadn't because she'd never known her mother to refuse anything sweet. So she sat there, with everyone's eyes on her, wishing she could sink through the floor.

"I'd love a piece, Cory." Zac's voice cut across the strain. "Chocolate cake is my favorite. I can't bake it and I never buy it because I'd eat the whole thing myself. But it's your birthday and I'm splurging. Make it a big piece." He held out his plate.

Cory's friends echoed that response, and soon most plates were heaped with Brianna's chocolate confection. Except her mother's.

"It's really good, Grandma. Couldn't you try a little piece?" Cory begged.

"No, thank you, dear. I'll just watch you all enjoy it. I understand that your mother forgot about me. After all, she doesn't see me much, does she?"

On and on the complaints went. Brianna tried to ignore

them but her father's pleading look forced her to return to the kitchen and scour the fridge for something for her mother. She scooped out a bowl of raspberry gelatin.

"Perhaps you'd prefer this," Brianna said setting it down in front of her mother.

"No, thank you. We have that every day at the home. Don't fuss about me," her mother said in a suffering tone. "I've gone without many times."

There was simply nothing to do but try to enjoy the rest of the evening. Cory loved the biking gear his pals gave him. He looked intrigued by the book on surfing, which Zac offered. He yelped with excitement when he opened the game system Brianna had chosen. But his biggest response came from the check his grandmother gave him.

"Five hundred dollars?" he squealed. "Wow! Thank you." He hugged her and she hugged him back. "I can do a lot with this."

"Honey, remember the rule." Brianna had always insisted Cory put birthday money into a special account, half for future schooling, and half to save for something special. But as she noticed the speculative gleam in her mother's eyes and the way she looked from Cory to herself, Brianna let it go. Later she'd have a talk with her son. "That's very generous, Mom and Dad," she murmured.

"Actually, that's from your mother. My gift is out here. Follow me." Her dad, his grin a mile wide, proudly led the way to the back porch and when everyone was there, swooped the blanket off a lump which turned out to be a restored remote-control airplane.

"Cool, Grandpa." Cory's jaw dropped.

Brianna couldn't help but smile when her father hunkered down to explain things to Cory and his friends. He looked ten years younger.

"It doesn't look very sturdy, Hugh," her mother whined. "It will probably crash the first time he flies it."

"It's a wonderful gift, Dad," Brianna said, delighted when her father's dimmed joy returned. At that moment she couldn't take one second more of her mother's negativity. "I'll get us all something to drink," she said, and hurried back to the dining room, wondering why she'd ever thought coming home would work.

"I'll help you clear." Zac spoke from directly behind her. With an ease that spoke of his previous job in a restaurant, he stacked the dirty dishes while she stored the leftovers. "I'm actually pretty adept at making coffee, too," he offered.

"Go for it. Strong and black," she muttered, inwardly seething at her mother's behavior.

"It's a nice party," Zac said as he set aside the extra napkins with *Happy Birthday* printed on them. "You have a knack for creating them. You're also a very good cook. That chicken was amazing."

"Thank you." Brianna sighed. No point in punishing Zac because her family was so messed up. "Thanks for giving Cory that book on surfing in Hawaii. Maybe something in it will finally spark some interest in him."

"He sure asked a lot of questions when he returned my book." His hand brushed hers as he helped load the dishwasher. His touch set off a chain reaction in her nerves.

"I guess I picked it up with my packages. Sorry." She closed the dishwasher door and edged away, wishing Zac didn't always have this stupid effect on her. "But that wasn't my only mistake yesterday. It seems I also bought a book without knowing it."

"Oh? Any good?" He leaned against the counter and watched her, which made her even more uncomfortable.

"Actually, yes. It's got me thinking about a whole new perspective on God."

"That's a good thing. Isn't it?" His dark eyes followed her as she pulled out cups for the coffee.

"Yes, it is," Brianna agreed, swallowing hard. Why did Zac still have to be so good-looking? She put the mugs on a tray, added the cream and sugar and drinks for the boys and her mother while she struggled to come up with a way to ask what was on her mind. Finally she just said it. "Zac, have you given any thought to doing something with Cory?"

"No." His relaxed look disappeared. "Not yet."

"I'm not trying to push you, but I am getting really concerned. There was an odd smell in the garage last night. I think someone was smoking something. Aside from those two—" she jerked a thumb over her shoulder toward the porch "—Cory doesn't seem to have made any other friends. When I ask, he won't talk to me about it." Brianna watched Zac's long lashes droop down, hiding the expression in his eyes. "I'm really worried about him getting into trouble," she whispered. "Cory's got to turn things around and he only has until Christmas to do it. I can't stand by and let the judge send him to detention. I just can't."

Brianna hated that she sounded so desperate. She was a child psychologist. She was supposed to know how to deal with kids. She should certainly be able to motivate her own son.

"I'll come up with something," Zac promised, his soothing tone smoothing her irritation. "Don't worry about it."

"He's my child," she whispered. "I can't help worrying."

Zac's eyes narrowed as his gaze met hers, but he nodded as if he understood. He studied her for a few more minutes before he spoke, his voice quiet but determined.

"I need to apologize for losing my temper with you. It wasn't your fault I was terrible at that presentation. I shouldn't have taken my anger out on you. But my lousy performance proves one thing."

"It does?" Brianna frowned. "What does it prove?"

"That I should not be in the forefront of Your World. Any more public stuff and I'll take a backseat. Agreed?"

"But, Zac, that was one time. You can't give up—"

"Hey, Zac. Come and look at this." Cory's voice echoed through the house.

"I guess we'd better get out there." Zac picked up the tray and headed for the porch.

Brianna followed more slowly with the coffee and a pitcher of iced tea, her heart whispering a plea to the only One who understood how much she wanted to help Zac, Cory and any others He set in her path.

"This movie is awful."

Mentally, Zac totally agreed with Cory's assessment.

"Why don't we shut it off and make some dinner," he suggested, glad when the boy quickly surged to his feet. "I'm starving."

Their night together two weeks after Cory's party wasn't off to a great start. Zac knew he had to do something. Since Cory had asked him numerous questions about grilling and other cooking skills, Zac decided to show him how to use the barbecue to cook meat, veggies and even dessert.

"You could make this on your own," he suggested later when the boy had cleaned his plate.

"I don't think I could make this."

"Practice makes perfect," Zac assured him. He reminded Cory of how easy it had been to prepare everything. "You could give your mom a break from cooking. She'd like that, wouldn't she?"

"I guess."

Zac heard something unsaid in that weak response, so he probed for more information.

"Doesn't she want you to cook?"

"She'd probably like it. She's kind of tired lately." Cory didn't look at him.

"Is she sick?" Zac held his breath waiting for an answer. How stupid was that. As if Brianna's health was his issue.

"No. I think it's about work. I heard her talking on the phone to some parents last night. It sounded like they were really mad at her." Cory carried the used dishes to the counter and began stacking them in the dishwasher.

"I wouldn't worry. Your mom is very good at negotiation. She used to talk my mom into lots of things when we were kids." Zac smiled at the memories.

"I heard you were friends with her." A bitter tone kept Cory's voice surly. "Of course my mother never told me about it. I didn't even know I had grandparents until we were moving here."

"Some people don't like to talk about the past." Zac wondered why Brianna hadn't bothered to tell her son about her own childhood.

"Mom never talks about the past. She changes the subject when I ask." Cory leaned against the counter as he spoke. "I think she kept everything a secret from me deliberately."

"Maybe she did," Zac defended. "But I'm sure she was only doing what she thought was best for you. After all, she's a single mom trying to raise you and do her job. It can't be easy."

"I guess not." Cory poured himself a glass of water and sipped it. "After my dad died, she took as many courses as she could from home, so she could stay with me. I remember getting up once for a drink of water. It was really late. She'd fallen asleep on top of her books." He took the utensils Zac handed him and began drying. "When I went to school, she went to college. But she was always home before me and if I had a sick day, she stayed with me and caught up her stuff the next day."

"Your mom sounds like she did a lot to give you the best life possible. You are the most important person in her world, Cory. That's why she's tried so hard to make a good life for you." Zac wondered what was beneath the boy's comments.

"Maybe." Cory dried the items, stored them in the drawer, then returned to his water.

"Maybe?" Zac frowned. "You don't think your mother loves you?"

"Yeah, she does. But—it doesn't make sense," Cory blurted out when the silence stretched tissue thin.

"What doesn't?" Zac dished out two cones, handed one to Cory, then led the way to his patio.

"Having me to look after, it was hard for her. I could see that. But now I realize she didn't have to do it all herself. I have a grandmother and a grandfather! They would have helped her, I know they would." Anger brought red dots of color to his cheeks.

"Cory, you don't know what happened back then," Zac interrupted but Cory wasn't listening.

"Everybody had somebody for Christmas. A family. An uncle, an aunt, grandparents. We never did. Mom and I went to church like all the other families, but we always came home alone."

Since he'd done the same thing after his mother's death, Zac's heart ached for the hurting boy. "I'm sorry."

"So am I, but so what? Mom could have changed that and she didn't." Cory's bottom lip jutted out. "If we had moved here when I was starting school, I'd have had a family for all the special times. I'd be like all the other kids. I'd have fit in. Instead I'm the oddball."

"Well, living here didn't help me much," Zac confessed, suppressing his reticence to try and help Brianna's child. "We moved to Hope when I was five, after my dad died in a car accident. But I never fit in. I was the oddball around here for years."

"But then what? You finally figured out how to fit in?" Cory frowned at him.

"No." Zac did not want to list his insecurities, but for the first time since he'd met Brianna's son, he saw real interest flare in the kid's eyes. He couldn't ignore the opportunity to engage him, because Brianna had asked him to do just that and there was no way Zac would let her down.

"Then?" Cory prodded.

"After a while I figured out that it didn't matter what other people thought about me, I had to be myself." Zac shrugged. "So I did my thing and eventually I found some friends. Kent, your mom, Jaclyn, Nick Green, Shay Parker. We learned that each of us had something special to share with the others."

"Hokey." Cory tilted his nose in the air.

"Maybe." Zac shrugged. "The point is I was still a nerd, Cory. But with my friends, that didn't seem to matter so much because we cheered on each other, helped each other reach our goals."

"You didn't cheer on my mom while she worked on her goal to be a psychologist." Cory glared at him. "You couldn't have. Because I never even heard of you till we moved here."

Zac hesitated. He did not want to get into the past. With anyone. If he told Cory the truth, the kid might start to think his father had been second best or worry he was second best. Neither were true. Brianna had dumped Zac and by doing so, made it clear to everyone that he didn't meet her expectations.

The sting of that still burned.

"You're not going to tell me the truth about the past, either, are you?" Cory snorted his disgust. "Because I'm a

kid who can't understand. Everybody thinks kids don't de-
serve to know the truth. Well, I know the truth. Grandma
told me you and my mom were going to get married but
my mom messed it up."

Aghast that Brianna's mother had spoken to Cory about
the past, and maligned her daughter in the process, Zac
gulped as he searched for a way to end this.

"That's not exactly right, Cory. Your mom and I were
engaged in college but we broke up. That was a long time
ago. People change. Things change."

"Why did you break up?" Cory's eyes bored into him.

"Our past is between us—private." Zac had to end this,
and fast. Revealing personal details was not part of helping Cory. "If you want to know more you should ask your
mother. She will tell you what she wants you to hear." He
almost felt sorry for the grilling Brianna might have to endure from this kid.

"You think she'll tell me about your past? Like she told
me about my grandparents? I doubt it." Cory's mutinous
face reflected his scorn. "I'll ask Grandma. She doesn't
think I'm a dummy. She always tells me the truth."

"Does she?" Zac asked quietly, then left it hanging, hoping those words would raise some doubts in Cory's mind.
"It's getting late. I'll walk you home. I missed my run
today."

Cory trailed him to the door, pausing to graze one finger over the book on South America. "Are you planning on
taking a trip there or something?"

"Yes." Zac held the door open and waited for him to walk
through. "Actually I'm hoping to use my Christmas holi-
days for a trek down the Amazon. I need to do a little more
research first, though. I like to really study a place before I
go there. Gives me more appreciation for it."

"From the look of all your pictures you've gone to lots of places," Cory mused, trying not to sound too interested.

"Quite a few." Zac listed several treks. "Haven't done the South Pole yet so that's on my list of to dos." Because Cory seemed interested, he told the boy a little about the places he'd seen. "I want to go back to Hawaii, too. I love it there."

"I knew some kids in my old school that went to Hawaii. They had awesome pictures." Was there a hint of longing in the boy's voice? But he said nothing more and they soon reached his home.

"Well, thanks for sharing my dinner, Cory. Sorry the movie was a bust."

"That's okay." Cory raced up the three stairs to the house and yanked open the door. "I'm not big on horror flicks anyway. See ya."

Zac turned to leave.

"You rented a horror movie to show my son?" Brianna emerged from the side of the house, lips pursed tight, fingers taut around a small metal weeding tool. Her short hair curled in damp wisps around her gorgeous face.

"No!" Startled, Zac regrouped. "I mean, I did, but I didn't know it was horror! Cory didn't tell me that when I asked him what he wanted to see. Anyway, we shut it off because it was boring."

The steely sparks in her change-color eyes lost a bit of hardness. She sighed.

"Sorry. I didn't mean to jump. I'm just a little on edge today."

"Cory said you were getting flack from some parents." He watched the tiredness bow her slim body. "The Larsens again?"

"And two others whose kids are beginning to talk about doing something with their lives other than maintaining the family business." She stared at him as if to remind him that she had done the same thing when she was their age. "What am I supposed to do? Tell the kids to forget their dreams?" Brianna made a face as she shook her head. "Forget I said that. Everything is supposed to be confidential."

"I can look it up in their records," he reminded her, glancing around. He couldn't prove it, but he had a hunch Cory was somewhere close, listening to them. "You look beat. Want to go for a milk shake? I'm buying."

Brianna blinked, her eyes huge below her spiky bangs. "A milk shake?"

"Pearson's still serves them, you know. With real whipped cream." When it looked as if she'd refuse, he leaned nearer and murmured, "I need to talk to you. Privately."

Brianna caught on immediately.

"A milk shake sounds excellent." She glanced behind her, nodded and said, "I'll make sure Dad doesn't have to go out again so he can stay with Cory."

"I'm not a baby, you know." Cory's indignant tones burst through the open window. "I don't need a babysitter."

"I'll be a minute, Zac. I'll bring my notes for Your World, too." She winked. "You can tell me what you think of my latest ideas."

"Great." Zac waited as a short discussion inside whispered through the walls. A few moments later Brianna walked through the door, a sweater in one hand and her bright turquoise bag in the other.

As they walked away from the house, Zac kept the conversation going with mundane comments but once they were a block away, Brianna laid a hand on his arm.

"You want to talk about Cory," she said.

"Yes." He couldn't help but notice how quickly she removed her hand. "Am I that obvious?"

"Well, you haven't asked me to go for a milk shake in

quite a while," she teased then quickly sobered. "What's wrong?"

"Not wrong exactly." As usual, the words deserted him. He pointed toward Pearson's. "Let's get our drink and take it to the park. We could talk there without anyone overhearing."

"Okay."

Once they were seated on a park bench, Brianna turned to him, expectation lighting the green of her eyes to a translucent glow. This was not going to be easy.

"Brianna, this is absolutely none of my business and it isn't easy to ask, but—" Zac exhaled "—do you think it's possible Cory resents you?"

Chapter Nine

"What did you say?" Brianna's jaw sagged.

She'd imagined a thousand scenarios for this "date" with Zac, and not one of them even came close to this.

"I said—"

"Never mind. I heard you. But I don't understand why you would think my son would resent me." Anger bubbled up at the injustice of it. "I've never done anything but my best for Cory."

"I don't doubt it." Zac fiddled with his straw. "And I am not accusing you. It was something Cory said. He'd been asking questions about our past relationship. He said your mother told him we were engaged but our breakup was your fault."

"Oh, no." She felt the blood drain from her head. *How dare she!*

"Then he got into memories about all the Christmases you two spent alone when you could have been here, sharing them with his grandparents."

Brianna listened as Zac related Cory's comments, trying to hide her pain. She worked so hard to keep her precious boy away from the misery her mother had imposed on her own life, and now Cory thought she'd cheated him out of a family? He resented her for saving him from the very things that had marred her own life?

Betrayal burned deep. Despite her best attempt, Brianna couldn't stop the tears from welling or dribbling down her cheeks to her chin.

"I'm sorry," Zac murmured. "I never wanted to hurt you. I just thought that if you knew—" His words faded into the shadows of dusk.

Brianna sniffled, glad that the sun had gone down, that here in the dark, no passersby would see her weeping. Because she couldn't stop.

"It's not fair," she mumbled.

"Oh, Brianna." Zac's arms came around her, and he hauled her against him, cupping the back of her head in his hand and drawing it against his shoulder. "I'm so sorry. I shouldn't have said anything."

"Yes, you should have." She dragged one hand across her face to erase the tears and leaned back just far enough to glare into his eyes. "Just because it hurts doesn't mean it isn't the truth. I have kept Cory away from Hope, deliberately. I had to."

"But, why?" His face conveyed his confusion. "Would it have been so terrible to come home for Christmas? Or invite your parents to Chicago?"

She reared away from him, incredulous that he could even ask.

"You've heard my mother, Zac. She can't stop criticizing me."

"Now, yes, it is bad," he agreed. "But that's her disease talking."

"No, that is my mother talking. That's how she's always been." She saw his disbelief and laughed, though there was no mirth in her eyes, only misery. "Why do you think I wanted so desperately to escape this place after high school?

Why did you imagine I begged you to tutor me so I could get a scholarship? I couldn't stay here, work in her store and get ground down anymore. I had to get away."

"You never told me this before." He frowned, fiddling with the curls at the nape of her neck as he tried to puzzle it out. "You never said a word. We were supposed to be married and you never confided any of this."

"Of course not. Do you think I wanted your pity? Your mother was perfect." His touch disconcerted her into saying more than she meant to. "Why did you think I never wanted to come home to be married?" Brianna demanded.

"I don't know." Zac looked into her eyes, searching for answers. "Why didn't you?"

"Because I knew she'd take it over," Brianna blurted out. "And she did. It wasn't our wedding. It was her chance to show off."

"That's why you changed everything from the small simple affair we'd originally decided on?" He sighed at her nod. "I thought it was because you regretted opting out of a big wedding."

"I never wanted a big wedding and I didn't change anything. She did," she murmured, edging her head away from his fingers. It was that or lay it against his shoulder and she didn't have the right to do that. Not anymore. She stared at him, glad the lamp overhead was dim enough to offer some protection from his searching eyes. "I just wanted to be married to you. I wanted us to be happy."

Zac opened his mouth to say something, but closed it again. Brianna let out her pent-up breath, realizing in that moment that she wanted him to say he wished they'd gone through with the wedding. But Zac didn't say that.

Instead he accused, "We should have talked about all this back then. You should have told me."

That was not what she wanted to hear. Brianna edged away from him, struggling to regain her composure.

"Like you should have told me about the job she offered you, preferably before you accepted it."

"Yes," he admitted. "I should have. But at least you learned about it. I didn't know about your mother and I should have. We shouldn't have had any secrets, Brianna."

Bitterness suffused her soul.

"No," she whispered, "we shouldn't have. But we both did."

"I didn't." He met her glare and frowned. "You're hinting at something but I don't know what. Why don't you tell me why you left? Be honest."

For a second, for one silly moment, she'd let herself imagine that Zac still cared about her, that they could recapture the feelings of the past. But she knew that wasn't true. The past was dead and gone, and just because she was weak and leaning on him now didn't mean anything had changed.

"I am always honest. Are you?" She shifted so his arms fell away from her, unable to bear his nearness and the memories it evoked.

"What does that mean?" he demanded with indignation.

Don't go there, Brianna. The pain isn't worth it.

"Forget it, okay? This is about Cory. I have to help him or he'll ruin his life." Resolve firmed her traitorous response to him. "I am not going to let that happen. You asked me why I didn't come back home. The truth is I never wanted to come back, except to work at Whispering Hope Clinic. If I could have kept my vow to Jessica and done it somewhere else, I would have. But she died here and I promised her I'd come back, help other kids through the pain of their worlds." She gulped. "My past is something I never want to return to again. But I'll tell you this, if I had to do it all again, I would do the same thing, to protect Cory."

"Have you no good memories of Hope?" Zac asked softly.

"Not enough to outweigh the misery." She refused to give in to the soft, squishy feelings that begged her to remember blissfully happy times in Hope—happy because Zac was there. "Coming home back then—I fell right into my mother's hands. And nothing has changed since except that now her focus is Cory. She'll do everything she can to alienate him from me, including cast doubt on my ability to parent. But my job is still to protect Cory."

"I think you're going to have to explain your decisions to him. He doesn't understand why you did it and he needs to. Plus, he's very fond of his grandmother," Zac reminded her.

"Of course he is." Brianna smiled bitterly. "She gives him everything he asks for. He has no boundaries with her."

"It must be hard for you to watch how she is with him." Zac's quiet words showed her he understood more than she'd expected.

"I'll live. The thing is, I have to walk a fine line between telling him the truth and destroying the relationship he's building with her. I don't want to do that, but neither do I want my son corrupted. Cory only has till Christmas to prove himself. I've got to ensure he does that without any more screw-ups." She rose and tossed her half-full cup in the trash. "Thank you for telling me, Zac. I have to think about it for a bit before I talk to Cory. It's delicate."

He, too, rose and walked beside her down the street without speaking. The entire time they'd been seated on the bench, people had been walking past. Brianna had no doubt that by tomorrow the entire town would be speculating on whether they were getting back together again. Let them. Right now she had to concentrate on her son.

"I'm glad we talked, Brianna. I think we should do it again. What you told me tonight raises a lot of questions about the past—our past." Zac stopped at the end of her walk, studying her through the gloom. "There are so many things I don't understand."

"Join the club." Like why he'd sided with her mother against her. Like why he'd been so willing to abandon everything they'd planned. Brianna pushed away the past, its questions and the pain. Time to move on. "Thanks for your help," she said. "Good night."

Zac nodded but said nothing. He stood in place, watching until she'd mounted the stairs. But as she drew the door closed behind her, Brianna thought she heard him murmur, "Till next time."

She fingered the ring at her neck as she closed the door on Zac and the rush of hope his words brought. There could be no next time for them, except as coworkers. She walked upstairs. Cory was in his room, hunched over the book Zac had given him.

"How was the milk shake?" he asked, his eyes hooded so she couldn't read his thoughts.

"Okay." She decided to say nothing about the mess surrounding her. Not tonight. "Is your homework finished?" she asked as she bent to brush a kiss against the top of his head.

"Yes, Mother," came the droll response.

"Good work. Good night, sweetie. I love you." She waited a second but Cory didn't respond with his usual "love ya." And that hurt. Before he could see her tears, she walked out. But in the security of her room she finally broke down, weeping her mother's heart out to God.

Even when she'd tried so hard to do the right thing, she'd hurt Cory. And praying about it brought little solace.

Her Bible lay open on her nightstand. The words leaped out at her.

Lord, why are You standing aloof and far away? Why do You hide when I need You the most? Why have You forsaken me? Why do You remain so distant? Why do You ignore my cries for help? Why have You abandoned me?

The hurt and anger poured out of her soul toward heaven in a torrent of misery. Desperate to find some relief she picked up the book she'd been reading and looked over Job's words.

But He knows where I am going. And when He has tested me like gold in a fire, He will pronounce me innocent.

The book's claim that some hardships in life were to test and mature faith, part of a normal friendship with God, reminded her of Zac's garden plaque. She glanced at the book. *Will you continue to love, trust, obey and worship God though you have no sense of His presence?*

"I'm trying," Brianna whispered. "I'm trying so hard to trust Your promise that You will never leave me. Please help me."

Worn out, Brianna sat in her window seat remembering the feel of Zac's arms around her in the park. As she stared up at the stars, old familiar feelings for Zac, which she'd thought long dead, welled up anew; familiar feelings that had made her want to run to him, throw herself into his arms and try to recapture the love she'd once found with him.

But he didn't want that. He'd said it was better they'd separated.

There was no going back. So why didn't that weak spot in her heart understand that just because Zac comforted her, just because he said and did nice things for her and her family, didn't mean he cared about her? Just because her heart skipped a beat whenever he appeared, just because she thought of him constantly, didn't mean anything could come of it.

The past was over.

So why couldn't Brianna let it go?

Troubled by the things he'd heard tonight and by the questions Brianna's comments had raised, Zac stretched out his run until his lungs burned and his knees ached. But tired as he was, he could not rest.

Had Brianna's life at home really been that bad? He'd envied her high-school popularity so much, Zac had never really looked beyond her lovely house, her successful parents and her seemingly perfect life. But now bits and pieces of past conversations with her mother in the weeks before their wedding brought new questions.

Brianna has no sense about color so of course I had to choose the bridesmaids' dresses.

I hope you won't mind, Zac, but I changed the order for the wedding cake. Brianna just doesn't understand how to coordinate anything.

The comments piled up in his mind, little things he hadn't paid much attention to back then, but should have.

When they'd begun college, Brianna's style had blossomed into autumn shades of rust and orange and turquoise. Those colors reflected her vibrant personality. He'd always wondered what prompted the change, though he'd never asked. Now he wondered, was it because she'd finally escaped her mother's dominance?

His overpowering response to Brianna tonight shocked Zac. He'd wanted the right to confront her mother, to shield her from the pain, to protect and help her. But that way of thinking was dangerous. Because their past was over.

Yet tonight, for a moment when he'd held her in his arms, Zac had desperately wished it wasn't. He'd wished he had the right to kiss her, to help her with Cory, to be part of her family and help ease the burden she carried.

Stupid.

Zac made himself a cup of calming tea. He sipped it outside on the patio and watched the stars. He tried to think of everything but Brianna. But despite his attempt to relax, Zac found himself more on edge than ever.

Brianna didn't want him. She'd made that clear ten years ago.

Zac had thought God had done the same thing. Though he still went to church, though he talked a good line to Brianna, it was all a facade to hide the loneliness in his heart. Tonight that barren emptiness welled up more powerfully than ever before, threatening to consume him. He still envied Brianna her family, even with the trouble they caused her.

Better than being alone.

Zac tossed out his tea and hurried back to his office. Work would ward it off. It always had before. Surely if he could focus on the next step to his goal, he could get his mind off the ache in the middle of his gut that came from wanting what he couldn't have.

But hours later Zac still hadn't dislodged the memory of Brianna's tears rolling down her downy-soft cheeks, or the weary sigh she'd breathed into his neck.

Or the realization that it had never felt more right to hold this woman in his arms.

"Look, Peter, my job is not to squash your daughter's dreams. My job is to help her understand herself so she'll find meaning in her world. I'm sorry you're not happy with my counsel, but the fact that Eve is even thinking about her future is a huge growth step from where she was a month ago." Brianna watched her former schoolmate's face harden and inwardly sighed. *Me, again, God. Please help.*

"We can't afford her dreams," came the bitter response.

"You don't have to. Right now they're just dreams. They may change and she'll have to figure a way to achieve them. For the moment she's still exploring." She struggled to sound empathetic but authoritative. "But I caution you that to keep disparaging her dreams only expands the rift between you. If you could just listen to her, encourage her to talk, share her hopes—"

"Share them? Don't you get it? I'd give my heart for my kid to get her dream. But it just isn't possible." Peter Larsen jumped to his feet. "You can't counsel our kids to do what you did, Brianna, to abandon their families."

"That's not what I'm trying to do," she finished, wincing as the door slammed shut.

Almost immediately the phone rang.

"Brianna, you need to come to my office. Now. Right away." Zac sounded disturbed.

"I wish I could but I've got two more parent meetings this morning."

"It's urgent. It's Cory."

Oh, no.

"Is he hurt?" Panic grabbed her.

"No." Zac's voice sounded hard. "He's fine. It's not that."

"Then it will have to wait. I promise I'll come as quickly as I can, Zac. That's the best I can do." With that she hung up, but through her meetings she remained concerned by the angst in his tone. Peter Larsen had been a sprinter in high school, but surely even he couldn't have gone from her office to the division office to complain so quickly.

Brianna pushed everything but her work aside, using every mediation skill she'd learned to calm the angry parents while still supporting their children's goals and dreams.

By noon she felt deflated and certain she'd made little progress.

"Zac Ender called twice," RaeAnn announced. "He said he'd supply lunch if you could get over there now."

"Call and tell him I'm on my way, please." But as she drove over, Brianna felt utterly unprepared to meet with Zac so soon after that evening in the park. No one was in the main office so she walked directly to his door and stepped inside. "What is so urgent?" she demanded, sinking into an armchair.

"This." Zac pointed to the television mounted on the wall. He pressed a button on the remote in his hand and a picture of the globe board at the school appeared.

"You had a camera installed?" she asked.

"The school board had a security system put in," Zac confirmed. "Yesterday afternoon the last camera was installed. Watch."

For what seemed ages the picture never changed. Then three shadowed figures appeared. After some whispering, one stepped forward and scrawled something across a corner of the white board in huge black letters.

"'Your World sucks,'" Brianna read. She frowned as the figure turned away, but in that moment she glimpsed the insignia on one corner of his jacket. "I think I know that crest from somewhere," she murmured, trying to remember.

"Yes, you do," Zac agreed in a grim tone. He backed up, zoomed in and replayed the footage, honing in on the figure.

"Cory!" Brianna gasped.

"And his two friends." Zac played the video once more, but there was no doubt who was responsible for the graffiti. "He's ruined Your World."

"But—when?" she asked, gutted by the knowledge that her child had deliberately sabotaged her. "How?"

"This tape is from last night. It's time stamped around

the time we were talking in the park." Zac's bleak expression spoke volumes.

In that moment Brianna understood how deep his disappointment went. He'd invested Your World with his hopes for that state job and now it seemed all was lost. She knew why. In the present apathetic climate, other kids would pick up on Cory's negativity and ruin whatever chance there had been. Her anger toward her son flared. To deliberately do this when Zac had been nothing but kindness—this time Cory had gone too far.

"What should we do?" he asked.

"Call him in," she said, her voice hard. She checked her watch. "Lunch should be over. Phone the school and get him in here. Have the principal drive him if you have to, but get Cory here now to explain himself."

"Just Cory?" Zac's wide brown eyes expressed his surprise.

"He was the one who wrote on the board. He pays the price." Brianna was done with pussyfooting around her son's issues. Maybe if she acted now, she could stop this from reaching the judge in Chicago. "Do it, Zac." She waited till he finally picked up the phone and dialed, though her knees were quaking at the stare he set on her.

"What is the price Cory is going to pay?" he asked in a tentative tone when he'd completed his call.

"You're the educator, you decide. I'll go along with your judgment." She sat down to wait. "But you should know that I am way past giving Cory another second chance without insisting on stiff repercussions for his actions."

"Be sure, Brianna, because we have to present a united front to him."

As if he were their child. The words hung unspoken in the room.

"Whatever you decide is fine. Clearly what I've tried

hasn't worked. You'd better come up with something before he gets here." Because Zac kept giving her funny sideways glances, Brianna pulled out a file she'd shoved in her handbag before she left her office and pretended to peruse it.

At last Zac broke his stare and worked on resetting the video.

Less than five minutes later Cory sauntered into the room and asked, "What's up?"

"You are," Zac said. "Sit down."

Brianna found no anger in Zac's tone, saw nothing on his face to give away his thoughts. Only deep disappointment darkened his eyes, though no one but she would recognize that because she'd seen it before, the morning of his botched presentation.

"What are you doing here, Mom?"

"I asked her to come, Cory. I thought she should see what you were up to last night."

At Zac's words, a deep rich red suffused Cory's face. He looked away from her, shuffling his feet against the carpet.

"Just another reason to be ashamed of me, huh, Mom?" Cory's head lifted. He glared at her, his blue eyes icy with anger and frustration.

"I have never ever been ashamed of you, Cory. I always thought you were God's gift to me. But today—" She glanced at the television. "Today I'm very ashamed. Of myself. I thought I'd done a better job raising you."

Cory frowned, as if he hadn't expected her to shoulder the blame for his misdeeds. "But—"

"The proof is right here." Zac flicked the remote and they all watched as Cory defaced school property.

Brianna felt sick. How had it come to this? How could God be in this?

"Your tests show you have a high IQ, Cory, but I'm beginning to think they're wrong. I'm beginning to wonder if you're actually very stupid."

Brianna's head jerked upward at Zac's strong words. But she remained silent as his eyes chided her to remember her promise.

"Thanks a lot," Cory said.

"I'm serious. What kind of bright person, who is supposed to be making an effort to change themselves so they don't have to go into detention, damages school property? That's a criminal offense," Zac reminded. "Do you *want* to be locked up?"

"That's not going to happen." But Cory's bravado slipped just a little.

"Really? If I call the police now, you will be charged and put in jail. That will be the last straw as far as the judge in Chicago is concerned. I doubt he'll wait till Christmas to rule on your case." Zac shut off the television. "So I guess you've just run out of options."

"Mom?" Cory pleaded, staring at her with those doe-soft eyes that sent a dart straight through her heart.

"This isn't on your mom, Cory. This is on you and you alone. Your two friends were there, but they didn't deface the board. You did. And I have the video to prove it." Zac stared straight at Brianna, challenging her. "Your mother and I have agreed that I must decide your punishment. Brianna, go back to work. I'll talk to you later."

She rose hesitantly, but knew there was no other choice. It had to be done.

"Straight home after school," she said to Cory. "No friends, no television, no phone. Clean up your room and get your homework done before I get home. You may not go to the nursing home with your grandfather. You may not go anywhere."

"But, Mom!"

Brianna turned her back and left Cory sitting there, the hardest thing she'd ever done.

Zac stood by the door, holding it open. She paused long enough to study his implacable expression. His fingers touched hers for an instant, transmitting warmth and something else—hope? Then she walked away, leaving her son in her former fiancé's hands.

Jaclyn met her at the doorway of Whispering Hope Clinic. She took one look at her face, grabbed her arm and drew Brianna into her office. She quickly closed the door and said, "Something's wrong. Spill it."

So Brianna told her the whole awful story.

"I'm failing everyone," she muttered, bitterly ashamed of her uncontrollable world. "Cory, my clients, the clinic, my mother. Especially God."

"That's ridiculous." Jaclyn poured a cup of strong black coffee and set it before her. "Listen to me, Bri, and hear me well. You haven't failed anyone. You're doing your job here at the clinic and doing so well, you have more clients than you can see. The kids love you."

"Because they think I go against their parents." As she'd always rebelled against her mother, Brianna mused.

"Because you really listen when they speak," Jaclyn corrected. "Because in talking to you they find hope for the future. Because you care. Kids can spot a fake a mile off. They wouldn't be here if they thought that was you."

"Thanks. I appreciate the encouragement." Brianna blinked when Jaclyn pushed her back into her chair.

"Stay. I'm not finished." Jaclyn sat down across from her, her lovely face serious. "You never failed your mother, Bri. Not ever. You tried to do as she wanted, but your heart lay elsewhere. You followed it and that's a good thing. Look how God is using you here at Whispering Hope. I'm no psychologist," she said with a funny grin. "But I'm going to hazard a guess that your mother is being so miserable to you now because she realizes all the years with you that she's lost. And as far as Cory is concerned—don't get me started. Nobody, and I do mean nobody, could have done a better job of loving that child. But sooner or later, his choices are his own."

"I guess you're right. It just hurts that he'd deliberately sabotage me that way."

"Of course it hurts, but you trust Zac, don't you?" Jaclyn's stare was intense.

"With Cory, you mean? Yes, of course." The certainty was there in her heart. Zac would do what was right for her son. He couldn't help himself because that's who Zac was.

"Then you have to trust that somehow he'll reach Cory. Zac has a way with kids—you've always known that." Jaclyn waited for Brianna's nod. "Relax. Let him handle this. Support him in whatever he decides and stop stewing over it."

"I'll try." Brianna chewed her bottom lip. "I still feel like I've failed God, though."

Jaclyn was silent for a long time.

"I should get back to work." Brianna set her cup on the desk. "Thanks for the pep talk."

"I want to say something else." Jaclyn cleared her throat as her eyes grew moist. "You won't know this, but when I first came back to Hope I had a terrible time trying to accept that I couldn't work my way into God's favor." A wry smile lifted her lips. "I tried hard, believe me. Worked myself flat out."

Brianna waited, wondering where this was leading.

"One day I was reading in Psalms and I found this verse. It's been very precious to me ever since." She slid a tiny Bible out of her pocket, thumbed through the pages and paused. Her eyes met Brianna's. "It's the fourth chapter.

Just listen," she whispered. She inhaled then read, "'O God, You have declared me perfect in Your eyes.'"

You have declared me perfect. Brianna couldn't wrap her mind around those words. She was perfect in God's eyes?

"Amazing, isn't it? God loves us so much He wipes out our sin," Jaclyn said quietly. "To Him we are perfect."

The phone buzzed. RaeAnn announced Jaclyn's patients were waiting. So were Brianna's.

"You always amaze me, Jaclyn. Thank you. But now I've really got to get to work," Brianna said. She smiled. "Some kids need my help."

"So do your mom and Cory, and even Zac," Jaclyn said softly as she hugged her. "And Zac might be the neediest of all. See ya."

Having mulled over the verse in every spare moment throughout the afternoon, Brianna considered Jaclyn's last words as she walked home that evening.

Zac needed her? Really?

She picked up her pace, anxious to get home and prepare for another parents' assembly at the school this evening. Zac had been there for her today. She didn't know what he'd said to Cory, but she'd been at her wits' end and he'd offered to help. She'd accepted his help because she didn't know what else to do.

Tonight she'd help Zac however she could, because she owed him. But that was as involved as she could get with him. There could be nothing between them and it was time she stopped leaning on him.

Her heart had tricked her into believing it was possible to build a relationship with this man again, but her brain kept repeating that Zac hadn't trusted her once. He might not again.

As she fingered the ring lying against her collarbone, the one Zac had given her so long ago on a very special Christmas Eve, Brianna knew she had to suppress her longing to regain his lost love.

Because she wouldn't survive losing it a second time.

Chapter Ten

"Good evening everyone. Uh, welcome." Zac gripped the edges of the high-school podium and gazed at the assembled group of parents, his mouth as dry as the desert. All the public-speaking courses he'd taken were worthless. He still felt like a guppy out of water when he stood in front of people.

"Uh." He gulped, feeling his palms sweat. "We, er, I promised you that after implementing Your World we'd gather again to discuss any questions you might have. Th-that is the purpose of our meeting tonight."

Mentally wincing at his poor presentation, Zac explained the steps he hoped to take over the next few weeks as the program continued to unfold. He chose to read primarily from his notes, desperate not to look a fool in front of all these people. But the more he read, the more nervous he became and the more he lost his concentration and began making silly errors.

"So, in effect, we've maximated—er—" As muffled laughter broke out in the group, Zac's whole body went tense and he could not get the next word out. Everyone was staring now—gawking at him, the spectacle in their midst.

"Actually, Zac, I don't think we've quite maximated yet."

Suddenly Brianna was there at his side, grinning at him as if they'd planned this interruption. "In fact, I don't think we've even come close to tapping the potential our teens have hidden inside." She winked at him. "Can I have a turn now?"

Relief swamped him but he didn't let it show.

"I suppose. But only if you follow my notes," he managed, pointing to the sheaf of papers atop the podium.

Brianna glanced at the stack of notes, rolled her eyes and gave her head the tiniest shake. She leaned into the microphone and whispered, "Not a chance. Those notes are maximated."

The room erupted in laughter. The tension broken, parents smiled as she went on to detail the next phase. Zac would have preferred to leave her to it but Brianna prevented that by deferring to him on several points and including him in a question and answer session, which could have become nasty given the Larsens' and other parents' outbursts. Zac staunchly defended Brianna, glad when she coaxed them to admit that their children were benefitting from the goals of Your World. By the conclusion of the meeting, the situation had grown almost jovial as parents sampled the coffee and cookies Brianna had thoughtfully provided. Zac knew the evening was a success because of her.

"Thanks for bailing me out," he said when everyone had left them to tidy.

"I didn't bail you out." Brianna stopped what she was doing and frowned at him. "Weren't you watching? Didn't you see those faces when you began to talk about the goals and dreams that have gone up on the Your World board? Those people ate up your words of encouragement, Zac. Hope was visible here tonight. Because of you." Then she squinted at him. "By the way, when did the kids start writing their dreams on the board?"

"I saw it on the tape after I sent Cory home." Zac grinned. "They wrote right over Cory's graffiti. I phoned to tell you but you weren't taking any calls. Come on. You can see the board for yourself." He held open the door, waited till she'd exited the auditorium then switched off the lights. "I'll tell you, when the video showed Eve take the pen and actually write on that board, my heart was in my mouth. That took a lot of courage in the face of her parents' objections. Look." He motioned to the board and held his breath.

"I came in the staff entrance so I never saw—" Brianna moved closer to him to take a second look. She read off several of the comments. "Isn't it fantastic, Zac?" she whispered, touching his arm as she stared at him, her eyes filled with awe.

"Yes, it is." Zac bent and kissed her on the lips. "It certainly is," he repeated, stunned by emotions that swamped him.

For one infinitesimal second Brianna had kissed him back. Now she stepped away.

"Why did you do that?" she demanded, her voice choked.

"I don't know. Excitement, I guess." Zac shrugged, pretending nonchalance. "No big deal. Sorry."

Now he was lying. Because kissing Brianna was a big deal to him. He'd wanted to kiss her even before that night in the park. And now that he had, he wanted to repeat it.

But Zac had seen that glint of green fill Brianna's eyes before. He knew she was suspicious of him. He was going to have to tread carefully if he wanted to find out exactly why she'd left Hope the way she had.

"Aren't you excited?" he asked. "There's your client's dream." He pointed to Eve's signature.

I want to be a doctor.

"I s-see it."

"Are you crying?" He frowned at the stream of tears

flowing down Brianna's cheeks and caught one on a fingertip. Something about it did funny things to his heart—squeezed it so tight it hurt. He'd wanted her to be happy, not weeping. "Brianna?" He tucked a finger under her chin and lifted it so he could see into her eyes.

"Tears of joy," she whispered. "Eve struck a chord in my heart the first time I saw her high on drugs and miserable. Maybe because she's in the same sort of situation I was. She carries so much guilt for wanting to be free of her parents' demands, for not being what they want. She was afraid to dream of anything for herself. But now, she's taken the first step toward independence." Brianna accepted the tissue Zac handed her, and smiled at him through her tears. "It's amazing."

"So why does that make you cry?" He didn't get it.

"Because I've finally achieved the goal I set myself way back when Jessica died, the one I started when you agreed to tutor me in high school. I've been able to truly help a child and it feels wonderful." She started crying all over again, and there was nothing Zac could do but wrap his arms around her and hold her while she soaked his shoulder.

Tenderness crept through him. This precious woman had carried such a heavy load for so long. He thought of the long nights she must have spent when Cory was a baby, teething, sick, tummy upsets. He remembered Cory had mentioned falling and breaking an arm when he was in kindergarten. How frightened Brianna must have been. Who had she called to share her fear? Who had she leaned on when he began getting in trouble?

He knew the answer. Tall, vivacious, strong Brianna—she would have hidden the weak moments and pretended she was in control.

"It's okay," Zac whispered, his breath moving the short

wispy strands on the top of her head. "You're not alone anymore."

She stilled. The muscles in Zac's arms protested as she edged away from him to stand separate.

"Aren't I?" she asked in a voice so soft he almost didn't hear.

Those hazel eyes studied him with an intensity that made him nervous. There was that hint of something painful in the look she laid on him. And then it was gone. The old Brianna was back in charge.

"What happened with Cory this afternoon?"

"I read him the riot act. Then I gave him a job he'll have to do until Christmas break. He reports to me." Zac shoved his useless hands in his pockets and shrugged. "I hoped I made him face a few hard truths." He frowned at her. "Why didn't you ask him?"

"I did." Brianna arched one eyebrow. "All my son would tell me is that the two of you talked, he's being punished and you are both going to a male Bible study on Wednesday evenings."

"Oh, yes. I forgot to tell you about that. Cory has a lot of questions." Zac felt his face heat up remembering Cory's very personal question about Zac's faith journey. "His faith questions are bigger than I can deal with. Besides, his two buddies have agreed to come along."

"To a Bible study?"

"I guess they want answers, too." Zac gave her a wry look. "One thing I've learned in working with students is that when you don't have the answers, you go somewhere you can find them. So we'll go to a Bible study about Peter, the disciple who was a bit of a misfit." Zac tried to look as if the prospect of studying the subject with Cory didn't scare him silly.

"Does Cory feel like he's a misfit?" The diffident way Brianna asked showed her insecurity.

"Yes." Zac watched her wince. "I think that's part of the reason he's angry at you for not coming to Hope earlier. He thinks that if he'd grown up here, he would have fit in with the other kids. You have to talk to him, Brianna. Explain at least some of your decisions. Otherwise his mind will make up what he doesn't know."

"I'll do it tonight."

"Good. Would you like me to be there?" he asked.

"You? Why?" Her eyes opened wide.

"In case you need help. Or something." It sounded lame, even to Zac. But to his surprise, Brianna nodded.

"Actually I'd really like it if you were there. Lately Cory and I seem to butt heads on everything. Maybe if you were there to act as a buffer, he'd be more open." She smiled, a genuine smile that lit up her green-brown eyes and stretched her mouth wide. "Thank you, Zac."

"No problem. Let me lock up, then I'll give you a ride. Your car is still on the fritz, isn't it?"

"Yes." Brianna sighed. "And apparently not worth repairing. Just another expense I've got to figure out. I'll wait for you outside. I could use a bit of fresh air before, well—" She made a face. "You know."

"Be positive." As Zac hurried to notify the caretaker that he was leaving, he realized he was looking forward to facing Cory's issues head-on. Maybe with Brianna's help, they could explain the past to the boy, and maybe, just maybe, Zac would find out exactly what had derailed their wedding without having to question Brianna. He didn't want to hurt her by dredging up the past, but he did want to know the truth.

For years Zac had rationalized that their breakup was God's way of preventing him from making the biggest mistake of his life because God knew he wasn't the right husband for Brianna. Brianna was bold, vivacious and outgoing. He was the exact opposite, and if they'd married, he knew he would have held her back. Brianna was a people person and though Zac wanted to be, though he'd tried to be for her sake, he knew that she'd have stifled her outgoing take-charge attitude, would have held back from taking the limelight in order to save him from exposure to the public focus he hated.

He wasn't the man for her.

But that didn't mean he didn't still care about her. That's why he couldn't stand by and watch another student, especially Brianna's son, fail. The graffiti, Cory's latest self-destructive behavior, had forced Zac out of his comfort zone and into a Bible study in order to reach the troubled youth.

And all those silly yearnings for Brianna that haunted him would have to be quashed while Zac tried to help her son.

Brianna held her mug of peppermint tea against her cheek and breathed a prayer for help as her son flopped on the sofa.

"This looks a lot like some television intervention," Cory mumbled as he looked from her to Zac. "What's going on?"

"I'm worried about you, son. You have only till Christmas, just a few months until the judge in Chicago reviews your case. I'm afraid he won't like what he sees. Vandalism?" Brianna glanced at Zac, hoping she was saying the right thing. "What's wrong, Cory? And please tell me the truth."

"You want the truth?" Cory's face turned red. His eyes narrowed and his hands clenched against the sofa cushions. "Okay. The truth is that I had grandparents and you never told me. I should have known."

Brianna was about to defend herself when she saw Zac shake his head. She inhaled and focused on Cory, waiting for him to let out all his resentment and bitterness. He blamed her for the rift with her mother and laid the blame for the breakup with Zac squarely at her feet. The pain of his words bit deeply, but Brianna refused to give way to it. The wound had to be cleansed before it would heal.

When Cory finally fell silent, Brianna wasn't sure how or where to start. But Zac did it for her.

"Is that all of it?" he asked in a stern tone. "Have you finished dumping all your misery on your mother now?"

"For the moment." Cory's lips pinched tight in fury.

"Good. Then you can listen for a while." Zac leaned forward so his face was only inches from Cory's. "What happened between your mother and me ten years ago is none of your business."

"But—"

"You had your say. Now you listen." Zac waited for the boy's reluctant nod. "Yes, we got engaged in college. Yes, we planned to marry. We didn't. It doesn't matter to you what happened. That's our business. Maybe one day your mother will tell you. Maybe she won't. That's up to her. All you need to know is that she had her reasons for leaving Hope."

"But why not come back?" Cory asked, his voice modulated, pleading as he stared at her. "Did Dad know you had parents here?"

"Your dad knew all about me when we married. Everything. I never lied to him or kept secrets from him." *But he did from me.*

Brianna opened her mouth, then saw Zac frown. She knew he was right. This wasn't the time for that truth. But it was time for another. She had to broach the crux of Cory's unhappiness.

"What I should have told you is that I never came back because of my mother."

"Grandma? Why do you hate her?" Cory demanded, his tone accusing.

"This isn't a debate, Cory," Zac warned. "Your mother is confiding in you because you asked for the truth. The question is, can you be mature enough to hear the truth without jumping to conclusions or judging her?"

After a dark glare at Zac and several moments of contemplation, Cory exhaled. "Go on, Mom," he said in a quieter tone. "I'm listening."

"Your grandmother had a store years ago."

"I know. She told me all about it. It sounded amazing." Cory's eyes glowed with excitement.

"It was amazing. I used to go there every day after school to help." Brianna closed her eyes, pushed back the flood of memories and concentrated on explaining. "My mother was fantastic at what she did. I admired her very much. But I didn't have her gift. I was lousy at what she did. Probably because I wasn't interested in home decor. I always wanted to work with kids. When I told her that, she wouldn't listen. I tried to explain that I wanted to become a psychologist, but she couldn't accept that. She convinced Dad not to support me to go to college."

"But, why?" Cory frowned.

Brianna explained what she'd learned about her own grandparents.

"Gosh, this family is full of secrets," Cory grumbled.

She stared straight at the child who filled her heart and soul with meaning. She loved Cory so much.

"Anyway, it was very important to me that I leave Hope to get my education so I could one day come back to work in the clinic." She told him all about Jessica, how close they'd been, the deep painful loss she'd felt when they'd learned the illness might have been treated successfully if it had been diagnosed earlier. "We'd planned that clinic in high school, Jaclyn, Shay and I. A clinic for kids. Helping kids was my dream."

"You've always said that. Grandma didn't understand?" Confusion filled Cory's face.

"Think about your Grandma, son. Even now she's very determined. In those days she was almost driven by her desire to make a name for her store. But I wasn't good at the things she was, even though I desperately wanted to be."

"Oh." Her son frowned.

Brianna took Cory's hands in her own. After taking a deep breath she reached out with her heart to her son.

"I tried so hard to be the daughter she wanted, Cory. But I couldn't make her dream mine. She wouldn't support me. So I persuaded Zac to tutor me so I could win a scholarship to college. And I did. We went to the same college and that's where we decided to get married."

Brianna deliberately did not say they'd fallen in love and she knew Zac noted the lack. She glanced at her former fiancé once and found his intent stare fixed on her. That's when she knew she had to tell the whole truth, for Zac's sake as much as for Cory's.

"But then you decided not to get married?" Cory prodded, his face confused. He glanced at Zac then back at Brianna.

"Yes." This was going to be hard. "The night before our wedding, my mother offered Zac a job at the school. She had it all arranged that we would stay in Hope after we were married. Zac would teach, and I'd work in her store. When I wouldn't agree she told me I was holding Zac back, that he'd never get the degree he dreamed of."

Zac's eyes widened. "But—"

"She told me a lot of things and I believed her," Brianna

whispered, begging him to understand. She turned back to Cory. "I believed that if I didn't do as she asked, I'd lose Zac, that he'd grow to hate me. I was scared and filled with doubts. I didn't want to hurt him and I sure didn't want him to regret marrying me or grow to resent me. But I wanted so badly to keep my vow to Jessica."

"And so?" Cory prodded when Brianna got caught staring into Zac's troubled gaze.

"I finally agreed I'd work in the store. I loved you, Zac. I wanted you to be happy. That teaching job seemed to make you happy. So I agreed to give up our dreams." Brianna felt the old pain rise up inside. The words flowed out. "What else could I do? My mother wanted me in that store, and you went along with it," she whispered sadly.

"Because we needed the money." Zac frowned. "It was only going to last two years. We could have saved a good chunk and—"

"Two years wasn't enough for her. I knew it wouldn't be."

"What do you mean?" Zac demanded.

The time had come. She had to tell him the truth and trust he'd understand why she'd made the choices she had.

"Brianna?"

"The morning of our wedding," she whispered. "Do you remember when you told me you thought we should come back early from our honeymoon as thanks for the wedding I never wanted?"

"I remember you laid a strip on me for even suggesting such a thing."

"Anyway, right after we hung up my mother came into my room. She had a contract."

"A what?" Cory's forehead wrinkled in confusion.

"A contract. For me to sign to guarantee that I wouldn't leave her high and dry." She licked her lips. "It was a contract for five years."

"Five years?" Zac glared at her. "She said two—"

"I know. And you believed her. You wouldn't listen to me when I warned you. You rode roughshod over every protest I tried to make." She gulped. "You wouldn't believe me over my mother."

"But I never meant—" Zac stopped and simply stared at her.

"You didn't suspect she persuaded your mother to say she was too ill to travel for the wedding, did you?" She smiled at Zac's start of surprise. "Of course you didn't. You never clued in that everything was arranged before we got there. The job, all of it. My mother figured if she could keep you in town, I'd have to stay because we'd be married. So she dangled the teaching job in front of you, and you bit."

"Why didn't you tell me?" Zac's mouth tightened.

"Because you didn't trust me. That's why I left before the wedding." Brianna faced Cory. "I knew we'd never get out once I got involved in my mother's store. I believed that after five years, Zac would hate me for killing his dream. I wasn't strong enough back then. I didn't know how to fight my mother and I knew I couldn't live in a marriage filled with hate. So I left." Brianna focused on Cory who was staring at her as if he'd never seen her before.

After a few moments he blinked and the anger was back. "But later?"

"Yes, I always planned to come home eventually. But then your dad died and you got sick. You were really sick, Cory. I was alone and scared and didn't know what to do. So I phoned home to ask my mother for help." The tears Brianna had kept suppressed spilled out in spite of her best efforts. She dashed them away, angry that still, after so many years the memory could wound so deeply.

"So she came?" Cory asked hesitantly.

"No." Brianna paused, inhaled and gathered her strength.

"My mother told me that I'd chosen you and your dad over her and now I was stuck with my choice. She hung up on me."

Nobody spoke for the longest time. Brianna used the moments to gather her composure.

"What did you do, Mom?" Cory's voice was very quiet.

"I called the two friends who'd always stuck by me. Jaclyn couldn't leave but she asked her mom to come help me. Shay sent me some money to live on until your dad's estate was settled. I managed." She cleared her throat and looked Cory straight in the eye. "And I kept on managing. You were my sunshine, my rainbow and I had to make sure your world was okay. I suffered a lot from my mother's criticism when I was growing up, son. It was really hard for me. I never felt loved and I didn't want that for you. So I did my best to raise you with all the love I had. After my mother hung up on me, I vowed I would never come back here. And I didn't. Until the day my dad wrote and asked for my help. I couldn't refuse him."

Silence fell as her child digested her words. But Brianna wasn't finished.

"I deliberately kept the truth from you, Cory. Maybe I shouldn't have. I don't know. All I know is that I had to protect you the best way I could. Back then I didn't know how my mother would react to you, but there was no way I was going to risk her hurting you." She gulped. "So I stayed away and kept my secret. I never told you about them. I managed the best I could."

"But I love Grandma." Cory's face hardened.

"Of course you do. And she loves you. You make her smile." Brianna touched his cheek. "You're a wonderful, thoughtful grandson and you should be in each other's lives. I'm glad you make her happy."

"But you don't want to be in Grandma's life?" Cory looked confused.

"Maybe one day I'll be able to but right now it doesn't work," Brianna said simply. "She's my mother and I love her, but I can't seem to do anything right around her. You've heard how she talks to me. You've seen the way she gets upset whenever I'm around." Shamed that Zac had to witness this, she continued in a low voice. "I don't want her to have another stroke, so I stay away. You and Dad visit her. She loves that."

"But you're her daughter," Cory protested.

"I know, honey." She smiled as she brushed his hair off his forehead.

"There must be something—"

"There is. We can pray about it." She leaned forward and kissed his cheek. "I love that you want to help, son, but, please, for my sake, don't talk about this with either Grandma or Grandpa. It would make them sad, and I don't want to do that. Okay?"

Cory was silent for a long time. He studied Zac for several moments, then glanced back at her, as if he were trying to visualize them ten years ago. Finally he nodded. "Okay."

"Thank you. I appreciate your listening and understanding." She rose and pulled him into her arms for a hug. "It's late. You'd better get to bed."

"Yeah." Cory looked at Zac. "Why did you come here tonight?" he asked.

"To support your mom. She hasn't had much of that lately. Now that you've got your answers, maybe you can change that." Zac held Cory's gaze with his own until the two came to some mutual unspoken understanding.

"Good night." Cory walked to the stairs and took them two at time, pausing at the top. "Hey, Zac, can I ask you something?"

"I guess." Zac turned to face him. "What?"

"The other day I was telling the guys about the traveling you did and all those pictures you have." Cory sat down on the top step. "They were pretty cool. In my old school they had a travel club. Do you think we could have one here, too? If you showed those pictures, I bet that would drum up some interest."

"A travel club?" Zac glanced at her.

"I think it's a great idea." Brianna smiled her encouragement. "Cory, honey, why don't you ask some of the kids at school if they're interested? Maybe if you got a travel club formed, you'd be able to plan a trip somewhere."

"Hawaii, that's where I want to go." Cory jumped to his feet. "I could learn the hula." He swiveled his hips, humming a Hawaiian song as he went to his room.

"Well. His emotions run the gamut in such a short time. I'm exhausted." Zac's face was stretched tight. "I wonder if my mom ever felt like that."

"Often, I'm sure." Brianna gathered up her teacup as she debated her next words. "Thank you, Zac," she finally said.

"Glad to help." He met her gaze and held it but she couldn't read his expression. "It was…enlightening."

"I probably should have talked to you about this before."

"You probably should have," he agreed in a grating tone. "Like perhaps the day of the wedding, maybe right before you took off out of town?" A tic in the corner of his cheek gave away his anger.

"You still don't understand," she whispered, and turned toward the kitchen.

"No," he said, grasping her elbow and forcing her to turn to face him. "You don't understand, Brianna. I get the part about your mother, though I still think you should have told me."

"But?" There was more to come and she knew it.

"What I don't understand is how you could have so little trust in me. You were far more important to me than any stupid degree. I would have given up anything to make you happy." Zac slid his finger around her throat, caught the delicate silver chain in his fingers and drew out the diamond ring he'd given her. "Did this mean nothing to you?"

"Why do you think I've kept it all these years?" she burst out, furious at him.

"I don't know. Why don't you tell me?" Zac murmured as his other hand grasped her and held her fast.

"Why?" Brianna demanded bitterly. "You said yourself that our breakup was probably for the best. You should thank me for running away."

"Yeah, I probably should. So—thanks a lot," he said through gritted teeth. Then he kissed her. But before she could react Zac was walking out the same door her father had just walked through.

"What was that about?" her dad asked glancing from Zac to her.

"My mistakes," she whispered. "I sure have made a lot of them." Strangely she didn't feel the least bit upset about that kiss. Even more strangely, she wondered when it would happen again.

Chapter Eleven

"You've been avoiding me," Kent said.

"What are you talking about?" Zac replied.

"You, professor. What's up?" Kent set a hip against Zac's desk.

"Work. I haven't been avoiding you. I'm busy. See?" He spread his hands above the papers on his desk and waited for Kent to excuse himself, but his buddy didn't or wouldn't take the hint.

"What is that mess?"

"It's Brianna's mid-November report for the board regarding Your World." He shuffled the papers, searching for an item she'd missed.

"I heard there are a bunch of new clubs forming. Seems like you two have conquered the apathy in the school. How is Brianna? Haven't seen her for a while, either. The two of you are like recluses." Kent slouched in a chair and kicked the heel of his boot over one knee.

"We work, Cowboy." Zac held Brianna's notes up to the light. "What do these scribbles say?" he asked himself.

"You can't phone her and ask?"

"I don't want to call her." That admission cost Zac.

"Because?" Clearly Kent would not give up easily.

Exasperated, Zac told Kent what he'd learned about his almost-wedding day and Brianna's reason for her disappearing act.

"She's a widow but she still wears my ring on a chain around her neck. Explain that."

"Ask Brianna, not me," Kent remarked.

"Not going to happen." Frustrated, he glared at Kent. "I've got to get through this. Can we talk later?"

"No." Kent straightened. "It's Saturday. You need a break, and I need your help. You may recall Thanksgiving is next week, then comes Christmas?"

"So I've heard." Zac gave up and leaned back in his chair. "Help with what?"

"Decorating the church for Christmas. You volunteered for that, remember?"

"Vaguely." A dim recollection filtered through Zac's brain.

"Our mission today, yours and mine, is to take the girls to the Christmas farm and gather enough props to decorate the outside of the church, ready for the live Bethlehem production." Kent checked his watch. "We leave in half an hour. You in?"

"Girls?" Zac studied his friend suspiciously. "And by that you mean?"

"Jaclyn and her helper, Brianna. Problem?"

Zac opened his mouth to object, but one look at Kent's resolute expression changed his mind. "You won't leave until I give in so let's go." He rose, grabbed his jacket and led the way out of his office.

Maybe this was the opportunity he needed to finally face Brianna. It was foolish, but he missed her. The hours moved so slowly when he didn't get to see her hazel eyes brighten with amusement, or darken when she was irritated with him. He missed her voice and the way she constantly encouraged, made him feel as if what he did mattered. It had taken these weeks for his anger with her to fade away. Now all he felt was loss.

"You're too quiet." Kent unlocked his truck and waited while Zac climbed inside.

"Be warned that this may not go well. Our last meeting was a little—testy."

"When you kissed her." Kent grinned at his blink of surprise. "Brianna talks to Jaclyn. Jaclyn talks to me. You should try that, buddy. Or maybe just go with the kissing."

"Not a bad idea. Except—where would a relationship between us go?" Zac snapped his seat belt as Kent started the engine and reversed, steering out of the lot and toward Whispering Hope Clinic. "I'm counting on my work here to get me into state education. Besides, now I've learned what was really behind Brianna's decision to leave Hope—lack of trust in me. She didn't even tell me the truth about her relationship with her mother! That's pretty hard to accept."

"Is it?" Kent let the truck idle as they waited for some kids to cross the road. His blue eyes pinned Zac. "Isn't the real reason you accepted that job offer her mother made was because *you* didn't trust Brianna?"

"That's what she said, too. I don't get what either of you mean." Zac glared at him.

"Come on, professor. The rest of us figured there were issues between her and her mother in high school. You were closer to Brianna than us. You must have had an inkling something was wrong," Kent insisted.

"Well, I didn't. I thought she had the perfect life. Call me clueless."

"I've called you worse," Kent joked, then grew serious. "Even so, why wouldn't you have talked to your *fiancée* about her mother's job offer?" He shook his head. "I get a job offer, I know I'm talking it over with Jaclyn long before

I decide anything. You guys were on the verge of marriage. You didn't think maybe you should get your almost-wife's input?"

"Brianna couldn't find work, remember?" Frustrated with having to defend himself, Zac repeated the things he'd told himself for ten years. "Going back to school was expensive. We needed the money. Staying in Hope so she could work in the store made a lot of sense."

"Made sense to whom? And at what price—the cost of Brianna's dignity, her dreams?" Kent shook his head. "I think it all boils down to trust. You didn't trust her enough."

Zac opened his mouth to argue then stopped. In a way Kent was right. He *had* been afraid—that if he didn't get his doctorate he wouldn't measure up in her eyes, afraid that he'd never get to be more than nerdy Zac. Most of all, he'd been afraid Brianna would ask more of him than he would be able to give.

It was that last one that stuck in Zac's brain as they drove to the clinic. His PhD wasn't the issue. Putting it off until both he and Brianna had enough funds to return to school would have cost him some time back then, but he would have achieved his goal eventually.

The real truth was Zac had refused to acknowledge his own doubts before the wedding. He'd glimpsed security in that job and clung to it. The real truth was Zac had been terrified by Brianna's girlish dream of the two of them forging into the future with only each other to depend on. The real truth was he hadn't believed in Brianna enough so he'd grabbed the easy way, just as her astute mother had known he would.

"I didn't trust that she was as committed to her dream as I was to mine," he confessed aloud, stunned by the truth. "I didn't trust that her warnings about her mother's manipulations were in my best interest. I didn't trust her."

"So what we have is the two of you heading for marriage and neither fully trusts the other." Kent scowled. "Doesn't sound like a recipe for happiness to me. I'd say it's a good thing you two didn't get married."

"That's what I told Brianna a while ago," Zac admitted.

"But did you mean it?" Kent pulled up to the clinic and switched off the motor. "The thing is, Zac, lack of trust is a disguise for plain old fear. Fear burrows into the deepest part of you. It infects everything you think, every interpretation you make. It weakens you so much you begin to withdraw rather than take a risk. You keep to yourself, you don't get involved. You see where I'm going here?"

"Sort of." Zac frowned at him.

"Fear is insidious. People laugh, you assume they're laughing at you. Next time you see them, you don't smile. They don't smile back. Pretty soon you expect the worst of everyone."

Zac frowned. Was that what he did?

"Fear is what got between you and Brianna, Zac. And it's still getting between you and others." Kent's earnest tone begged him to hear the truth. "You have to overcome your fear that you'll draw negative attention, that you'll be on display and people will laugh. You have to give people a chance to see the real you."

Trepidation crept up his spine and closed around his skull. Let them see the real him? The insecure part that yearned to be loved? The thought terrified him.

"Stop worrying whether you'll say the wrong thing or give the wrong impression and recognize that everyone is struggling just as hard as you to figure out the path God has set." Kent frowned. "The idea is for us to help each other along the way, not to go it alone."

Zac mulled that over until Kent's chuckles drew him out of his introspection. "What's so funny?"

"Look at our ladies. I specifically said we would be walking over rough terrain." He inclined his head. Jaclyn and Brianna emerged from the clinic, both wearing high heels.

"You expected hiking boots? Fashion is king with those two." Zac watched them lock the clinic door, wave, then saunter toward the truck. His heart thumped an extra beat when Brianna's gaze rested on him.

"Our Bible study got me thinking," Kent said. "You're the reverse of Peter. He blabbed whatever came into his head, but you think too much about what you're going to say. Be honest, Zac. Speak to Brianna from the heart."

Easy to say. Hard to do. Zac got out of the truck.

"Hi, guys." After kissing Kent, Jaclyn stood on tiptoe and brushed her lips against Zac's cheek, her smile welcoming. "I'm so glad you could come. Will you mind squishing in the backseat with Brianna? I'd do it but the baby makes me carsick when I sit in the back."

"No problem," Zac agreed, slightly unnerved by Brianna's intense scrutiny of him.

"Great." Jaclyn beamed. "Cory's coming, too. He should be here in a minute. It's too bad we only have bucket seats in front. You and Brianna will be squashed." She accepted her husband's help to ascend the truck.

"Cory?" Zac glanced at Brianna.

"Oh, yes," she said, her voice tight. "He was talking to Mom about how she used to decorate the church inside and out, and now he thinks he's going to direct us to create the same result."

"Good for him." Kent waited until Zac and Brianna were seated in back. He stood waiting for Cory, who came across the lot at a run and flung himself into the backseat. "Everybody okay? Not too squished back there?"

"We're fine," Brianna said quickly.

Fine? With Brianna seated so close to him, Zac found it

impossible to mull over his best friend's words. He couldn't help but inhale the soft sweet gardenia scent of her favorite soap, or brush against her bright red quilted jacket when the truck bumped over road construction, or notice the flattering length of her knee-high boots as she eased her long legs into a more comfortable position. She was gorgeous.

"Do you have enough room?" he asked. Brianna's hair brushed his chin as she nodded. She kept her eyes focused forward.

"So, Cory," Kent said, "what have you been up to?"

"Library. Research." He shot Zac a look. "I made a really dumb mistake, so for payback I have to write some essays. I have to do two per week."

"What's the topic?" Jaclyn asked.

"Hawaii."

Zac could feel the heat of Brianna's stare. When he turned his head, he saw a funny little smile tug at her mouth.

"Very clever. He wouldn't tell me what his punishment was," she murmured, for Zac's ears only. "Hawaii is all he talks about now. Getting him to do even more research on it has kept him busy, and his friends are just as engaged."

"It's an awesome place." Zac had planned to take her there for their first anniversary. Instead he'd gone alone.

For the rest of the ride Cory deluged them with facts about the islands. They also learned that he'd persuaded one of his two friends to help with the church decorating. When they finally reached the Christmas farm and Zac climbed out of the truck, he felt oddly reluctant to have the ride end.

"Will you be able to load as much stuff as I want?" Cory asked, glancing from Zac to Kent.

"Uh, how much do you want, exactly?" Kent was careful to ask.

"A lot. Grandma gave me a list. It's pretty big."

"Honey, did you check with the pastor about this?" Brianna looked worried. "There must be a budget."

"There is. Grandma found out and wrote it all down. The pastor said nobody else had offered so we should go ahead and get whatever we see fit. Okay?" Cory was almost dancing with anticipation.

"Okay." Brianna nodded and he raced off. Kent and Jaclyn were close behind. Jaclyn shared Cory's vision for the decorating and was eager to help.

"So? Where should we start?" Zac studied Brianna's glowing eyes and bright cheeks.

"In the coffee shop? They're serving mulled cider." She shrugged. "Let's let them do all the hard stuff."

"My kind of volunteering." Zac walked with her to the entrance, found it bustling. "How can Christmas be just five weeks away?" he asked, amazed by the number of people present. "Seems like only days ago we started Your World."

"I know. And now it's taken off." Some of the glow left Brianna's eyes. After telling him what she wanted she hurried to claim a table before someone else grabbed it.

Confused by her reaction, Zac purchased their drinks along with gingerbread cake with whipped cream and carried the tray to the table. Something was wrong.

"What's up?" he said, when after several minutes Brianna hadn't touched either.

"I've lost Eve Larsen as a client. She said her parents refuse to let her see me anymore. They've had to lay off another employee and Eve will have to fill in the slack at the café." Brianna fiddled with her cup. "There's no way they could pay for even one year of college now. They're barely staying afloat."

"I'm sorry." Zac didn't know what else to say.

"So am I. But I can't blame them. She's not even finished school yet. Their priority has to be providing a living for the family." Brianna lifted her head, pretended to smile. "Eve said she's not letting go of her dream, just putting it on hold, for now. But even if she eventually found funding, I'm not sure she could abandon her family when they need her so badly."

"I'll do some checking into funding. And there's always a scholarship." When she didn't return his grin Zac sipped his cider and tried to decide on a way to broach his apology. Finally he just blurted it out.

"That day at your house— I'm sorry I blew up."

She looked at him, her face sad, her eyes shadowed. Then suddenly her shoulders went back and her eyes began to glow green with anger.

"You know what, Zac? I've had it with apologies," she said in the "tough mom" voice he'd heard her use on Cory. "I apologize for the past. You apologize for the past. We're always saying we're sorry. I don't need apologies anymore."

"Okay." Her vehemence surprised him. "What do you need?"

"Answers. Why did you go along with my mother and give up all our dreams?" She leaned forward, her face inches from his.

In that moment Zac knew there was no more hiding, no more pretending. He owed her the truth.

"I was scared," he admitted.

"You were scared?" Brianna blinked. "Of what?"

"You. You and me. That we wouldn't last. That I wouldn't be good enough for you. You're so strong, Brianna. You're outgoing and you get up there and inspire people and I, well, I don't. I get tongue-tied and flustered and the right words never come out. I figured you'd want me to change, to become someone more like you, and I knew I couldn't do it. I will never be like you." Haltingly Zac admitted the feelings he'd kept bottled inside for so long. "I envied you all through high school, you know. You were always so popular. You had everything I wanted. Even when we were making wedding plans, I couldn't believe you'd actually marry me. When you left I realized I'd secretly been waiting for it to happen."

"You didn't trust me, that I loved you as you are," she whispered sadly.

"Just like you didn't trust me," he countered, and reached out to brush a finger against the silver chain just visible at her throat. "We both let our secret fears ruin what we could have had." Zac withdrew his hand. He didn't know what else to say.

"I did love you." Brianna met his gaze and didn't look away. "I loved you very much."

"Why me?" He needed to know.

"Because you loved me as I was. Because with you I was enough. I didn't have to change anything about myself." A funny smile appeared. "I didn't have to pretend with you."

"And yet you did," he reminded. "You pretended your mother's choices about the wedding were okay. You should have told me they weren't."

"I know."

"And I should have listened to you. I shouldn't have pretended I was okay with you not being able to find a job. I was worried sick that we'd get into some kind of massive debt like my mom had because of my surgeries," he confessed. "Every day I watched how scrimping to get out from under that debt load stole her health. I vowed I'd never let that happen to me. That's why I was so quick to agree to your mother's suggestion. I saw a way out."

"You never told me that. And you should have." After several moments, Brianna shook her head and sighed. "So where does that leave us?"

"As friends?" he asked, his insides quaking at making such a bold request. "Friends who don't keep secrets? Friends who trust each other enough to tell the truth no matter what? Friends who'll be there for the other one whenever needed?"

"Yes." Brianna smiled shyly. "I'd like that, Zac. Friend." She held out her small hand.

Zac shook it with a rush of relief. But the moment his fingers touched hers, he wondered if friendship was going to be enough for him.

It would have to be, he decided. Because he wasn't husband material. That was the one thing their breakup had taught him. He would never be any different than he was now. A nerd. An oddball. He didn't want her to be ashamed of him. Of course, knowing that didn't negate the root of love that had snuck back into his heart. Brianna was still the only woman he cared about.

But acting on those feelings? No. Too much time had passed. She'd moved on.

Besides, he didn't dare tell her his feelings and risk her rejection. His throat clamped closed and his palms began to sweat as memories of his year of embarrassment and humiliation flooded in. He could not, would not, go through that again.

After they finished their snack, they headed outside and toured the Christmas lot. Brianna chose several things she wanted to decorate her house with. She paused beside a huge potted poinsettia.

"This is my mother's favorite flower," she murmured. She fingered a petal, lost in thought.

"How's it going with her?" Zac asked, hating that she'd lost her happy glow.

"I don't see her much," Brianna admitted. "Things always seem to go south when we get together and somehow, great psychologist that I am, I can't seem to stop it." She gave a self-effacing laugh. "All that education I worked so hard to achieve—wasted."

"I doubt it. But maybe what you need is a new approach," he said.

"Going to fix my mom as you fixed Cory, Zac?" Brianna teased. "He's like a different kid. What did you say to him that day in your office anyway?"

"Not a lot." Zac didn't want to betray Cory's confidences. "I laid out some cold hard facts and he manned up."

"Well, you did a great job," Brianna said. "I told you years ago and I'll repeat it now, you have a very special way with kids, Zac. I wish you weren't so set on leaving the best part of education for a desk job in a room where no kid will get the benefit of your gift."

"I don't know about any special gift, but I am still aiming to transform kids' lives. I'll just be doing it through curriculum," he defended.

"I know. And you'll be a success there, too." A small sad smile lifted her lips. "But it seems such a waste of a God-given talent. You start talking to a kid and before you know it that kid is responding, opening up, seeing potential in himself and possibilities. I wish you'd realize how much of a difference you make when you're with them one-to-one." She grinned, shook her head. "Never mind me. What I really wanted to say was thank you for taking an interest in Cory. He told me he has to report to you on several fronts."

"He's a good kid." He knew her mind wasn't on the task though because she moved from one display to the next without choosing anything. "So what else is bothering you?"

"Cory's working really hard to get the travel club going, but the other kids scoff at his dream of a group trip to Hawaii at Easter. I wish there was a way to snag their interest." She sighed. "But then I'm a mom. I just want to fix everything in my kid's world."

"Brianna, you always want to fix everything in everyone's world," he said, cupping her cheek in his palm. "That's what makes you so good at what you do."

"Why, Zac, what a lovely thing to say." She snuggled into his palm for a sweet moment.

The way she smiled at him sent Zac's heart into overdrive.

"Hey, Zac?" Cory's voice interrupted the moment.

"Hey. How's it going?" Zac dropped his hand, summoned a smile and tried not to resent Brianna's son for interrupting them.

"Good. Kent and Jaclyn are discussing some props. I was wondering if you could help me with something." Cory glanced at Brianna's feet. "You don't have to come, Mom. We men can handle it. Besides, it's rough ground, and you might trip."

"Thank you for your consideration, son," Brianna said, tongue in cheek. "I did want to check into getting a live tree for Christmas. Shall I meet you at the main building in half an hour?"

They agreed, and she wandered off.

Zac looked at Cory. "What's going on?"

"I wanted to ask you something and I didn't want her to overhear." Cory shuffled his feet.

Zac waited.

"It's about Mom," he said in a hushed tone.

"What about her?" Zac watched Brianna's red jacket move in and out of the booths surrounding the area. "Is something wrong?" he asked turning his focus back on Cory.

"She didn't tell you." Cory looked straight at him. "She's lost seven clients. Now some of the parents are trying to convince others to get keep their kids away from Whispering Hope Clinic."

Zac sucked in his breath and tried not to let his anger show. Brianna had gone above and beyond to encourage these kids, to get them thinking about their futures. And some selfish parents were going to ruin all her work? No way.

"What did you have in mind?" he asked Cory.

"Some kind of event that would show everyone the good she's done." Cory's blue eyes begged for help. "Please? I don't want us to have to leave Hope, but more than that, I don't want my mom to have to leave Whispering Hope Clinic. She loves her work there."

"Give me a couple of days to think about it, Cory. I'll come up with something." Zac had lost sight of the red quilted jacket. "Let's go over to those booths. I want to take a look at the ornaments."

"Why? I thought you were going to the Amazon for Christmas?" Cory stared at him.

"So? I'd still like to have some Christmas decorations up. I might even decide to have a party. I'd like something really nice." He was babbling. Thankfully Cory didn't seem to notice as he led the way to a booth with blown-glass ornaments.

"Mom loves these," the boy told him.

That was good enough for Zac. He ordered a grouping and paid to have them shipped.

"You're sure getting in the Christmas spirit." Cory blinked at the amount the clerk quoted.

"Yes, I am," Zac agreed. For the first time in years warmth filled his heart. Brianna thought he had a God-given talent.

He wandered through the stalls with Cory, thinking about that conversation with Brianna. Kent had been right, as usual. He did need to be more open. Look what it had got him—being friends with Brianna.

He liked the sound of that.

But a niggling little voice in the back of Zac's head reminded him of his accelerated pulse when his hand had cupped her face, warned him of his regret that he hadn't been able to pull her into his arms and hold her, as he'd once had the right to do.

Was friendship with Brianna going to make him regret they didn't share more?

Chapter Twelve

"I don't know why I ever agreed to do this."

The day before Thanksgiving, fear crept over Zac's handsome face. Brianna knew she had to do something to shock him out of his self-consciousness.

"You agreed because you're a wonderful friend who is trying to help Cory," she whispered. She stood on tiptoe to kiss him on the mouth. "Now go and show those kids the glories of Hawaii."

He nodded, turned and walked away as if in a daze.

"Some of you are considering joining the travel club," he said when the room had quieted. "I thought you might like to see just a few of the wonders you'll find if you go to Hawaii."

The room darkened. Brianna sat down at the back, prepared to intervene if Zac needed her. Instead she became transfixed by Zac's stunning pictures and by his easy commentary. Several times he had the room giggling, sometimes he commanded total silence, but not once did he lose his train of thought or stumble. This was a man bent on sharing his love of the islands. His passion infused everything he said. At the end of the presentation, Cory's sign-up table had a lineup.

"You did a fantastic job," she praised Zac when the cluster of kids around him finally left. "I think it was the cliff divers that sealed their interest."

"Those pictures are pretty good," he agreed, shutting down his computer.

She touched his arm to draw his attention.

"I wasn't talking about the pictures, though they are awesome. I was talking about you. You reached out and grabbed the kids' attention when you spoke. You had them eating out of your hand." She smiled. "That's one more reason you should be back in the classroom. You're God's gift to this school."

"That's twice you've called me God's gift. I'm getting a swelled head," he joked, a flush of red heating up his neck.

"Well, you can only be God's gift if you let Him use you," Brianna said. She studied Cory's almost full sign-up sheet. "All right! Let's go celebrate. My treat."

"Thanks, but can't do it, Mom." Cory shoved his papers in his backpack, hurrying to join the two friends waiting for him by the door. "We're doing a project together."

"Okay. See you at dinner," she called. She turned and found Zac studying her. "What project are they working on with him?"

Zac shrugged. "I have no idea. Whatever it is, he's very excited about it. I can't believe how he's changed."

"That's thanks to you."

"He did it himself. I just gave him a push."

"I hope they're not up to something bad—" She squelched the thought. "I'm sure they're fine. You do realize he's going to want you to act as chaperone when they get a trip to Hawaii organized." She frowned at him. "What?"

"Brianna, I'm covered in scars from the surgeries," Zac protested. "I don't want the kids to see that."

"So wear a T-shirt. Or don't. After the first glance, they'll be too busy taking in the sights to notice you." She waited. "Well?"

"You're very pushy, you know," he teased. "I'll think about it. Okay?" He lifted his laptop. "Did you mean it about that treat?"

"Sure. Why?" she asked, curious about the determined look on his face as they walked through the school.

"I want to discuss something with you."

"Okay." Ten minutes later Brianna ignored the coffee she'd been craving to stare at him, amazed by his genius. "A student fair," she repeated.

"A Your World fair," Zac corrected. "The last day of school before Christmas break. For students to showcase what they've learned. Here's what I've got so far."

Brianna listened, applauded his ideas and suggested a few of her own. It was a great idea that would maximize the students' successes. That was the thing about Zac. He was always looking out for the students. That's what made him a top-notch educator. If only he could realize his own potential.

"The last day of school before Christmas break?" she asked.

"Yes." Zac grinned. "Two reasons for that. The kids will go out on a high, and the parents will have the break to think over the results achieved. Maybe that will quash the nay-saying that's going on now."

"You heard," she said, embarrassed that her failures had reached his ears. He was probably regretting ever giving the school counseling contract to Whispering Hope Clinic.

"I hear most things," he said, studying her with a serious look. "There aren't many secrets in Hope anyway."

"I guess not." Brianna wondered if Zac knew that the old flame she'd carried for him had reignited. Did he guess that the feelings she used to have for him had grown and multiplied? Had she given herself away?

"So you're good with a Your World fair?" he asked.

"It's a great idea. It won't hurt for the state folks to hear about this, either, will it?"

"I never considered that, Brianna." Zac frowned at her. "This is for the kids and the parents."

"Oh, I know. But it can't hurt you to have them witness your success." She smiled to hide the fact that she hated to think of Zac leaving Hope. He'd become an integral part of her life.

"*Our* success." Zac pushed away his coffee cup. "And someone would have to tell them. I, for one, don't intend to do that. This should be a town-wide celebration." He checked his watch. "I need to get back to the office."

"Okay." She followed him outside then impulsively stopped him with a hand on his arm. "Listen, I know it's a bit late and you probably already have plans, but I was wondering if you wanted to come over tomorrow for dinner. I'm not the world's greatest chef but I think I can guarantee most of our Thanksgiving dinner will be edible. Unless—"

"I'd like to come. Thank you." He said it so quietly she blinked.

"Oh. Great." Surprised by his enthusiasm, Brianna got lost in his amazing eyes.

"What time and what can I bring? Brianna?" Zac shook her arm.

"We won't eat till later in the day," she mumbled, embarrassed that he'd caught her staring. "Come when you like and bring whatever you want. Or nothing at all. We'll have plenty of food."

"I know how to make an awesome salad," he offered.

"Perfect." Nonplussed by the intensity of his gaze, Brianna waved. "See you tomorrow."

"Yes. Thanks."

Brianna glanced back once, found him still watching her. Her stomach fluttered. Heat suffused her face. She suddenly had the urge to skip down the street.

I'm going to need some help here, God, she prayed as she walked home. *Zac's a nice guy, but he wants to be friends. I want more but he plans on leaving. Help me?*

As soon as she arrived home, Brianna changed clothes, then grabbed the book and her Bible and began searching for answers. The first words she read stole her breath.

Relationships are always worth restoring.

She'd already restored her relationship with Zac. It wasn't exactly the relationship she wanted and it would take time to rebuild the trust, but they'd made a start. She was also working to reestablish her relationship with God. So what—?

Her mother.

Immediately a sense of guilt and frustration filled Brianna. How could she possibly restore that relationship knowing that her mother had been integral to causing her unhappiness?

Forgive.

She didn't see the word on the page. Rather it was a soft sweet whisper in her heart.

Forgive. Start afresh. Restore.

Only with her mother?

Or could God possibly intend that her previous relationship with Zac could also be restored?

Giddy, scared and filled with questions, Brianna prayed.

"Let's eat everyone." Flushed and looking slightly off balance, Brianna waited as her father pushed her mother's chair to the table.

Cory sat on one side, her father on the other. Zac took the place next to Brianna, which wasn't a hardship. Lately he wanted to sit beside her more and more. Anything just to be near her.

"Dad, would you say grace?"

"Yes, of course. Let's join hands."

Brianna blinked. Zac reached out and grasped her hand in his. He loved the way her hand fit into his. His gaze caught and held hers. He smiled. Brianna smiled back.

"Happy Thanksgiving," he whispered so softly no one else could hear.

Her father started praying, but when he said, "Let a spirit of thanksgiving and love pervade this house on this day," Zac tightened his fingers around Brianna's. He wished he could make it so.

Because that was exactly what he wanted for her here in her old home. A spirit of love. A time when she would finally be appreciated for all she was. If God gave him the opportunity, he was going to make that happen. Brianna was a special woman who devoted herself to helping others. It was way past time her mother saw that others appreciated her daughter.

Zac felt her gaze on him. Her smile made his stomach twist.

Oh, Lord, I am crazy about this woman.

Brianna withdrew her hand on the pretext of passing food.

"Mom, this smells so good. I'm starving."

"Thanks, honey. I hope you enjoy everything." Cory's comment brought a soft glow of joy to Brianna's face, quickly doused by her mother's complaint that the turkey was too dry.

"I don't want to contradict you, Mrs. Benson," Zac said quietly, "but I think this turkey is cooked to perfection. And when loving hands prepared it, that makes it taste all the better. Don't you agree?"

Mrs. Benson's mouth formed an *O* of surprise. She glanced around and quickly nodded. "Yes, that's true. But the potatoes—Brianna always makes them too soft."

"I'm sure that's because Cory likes them that way. You probably did the same kind of thing, made food her favorite way when Brianna was a child, didn't you?" Zac asked smoothly. "I know my mom did. I guess that's what mother's do. They go all out for their kids, because they love them."

And so it went. For every complaint her mother voiced, Zac countered with another about family or love. Determined to stop this woman from ruining Brianna's Thanksgiving, by the end of the meal he thought he might have succeeded. Mrs. Benson's complaints had dwindled to almost nothing.

"I hope everyone left room for pie," Brianna said, rising to collect plates.

"I'll have to wait awhile," Zac told her as he gathered up serving dishes. "Everything was so good, I ate too much dinner."

"Me, too, Mom." Cory grinned. "I think I ate the most potatoes. They were so good."

"Everything was good," Mr. Benson said. "It was a delicious meal, honey. Don't you think so, dear?" he asked his wife.

"Well—" Mrs. Benson began to say something, glanced at Zac and nodded. "Everything was very tasty, Brianna. You did a good job."

"Thank you." Brianna's hazel eyes stretched as she stared at her mother. Finally she gathered herself enough to say, "You and Dad go relax with Zac. I'll just clean this up."

"Don't be silly. I'm helping you." Zac took the dishes from her hands as he glanced at Cory. "We all are. You did the cooking, we'll do the cleanup."

"Zac's right, Mom. We can do it. You take a break. Stay there." Cory poured her a cup of coffee, added cream the way she liked it, then grinned. "C'mon, Grandma. You can show me the right way to load the dishwasher."

"You mean you don't know?" she asked, frowning at him.

"No clue," Cory said with a wink at Zac.

"Then it's time you learned. I'm a firm believer men should be able to do for themselves. Look at Zac. He was able to make that salad himself, though I'm not sure the combination of—" She blinked at Zac then smiled. "It was a delicious salad," she said.

"Thank you, Mrs. Benson."

"Come along, young man," she said to Cory. She wheeled her chair into the kitchen with an energy Zac had never seen before. A moment later they heard her giving Cory and her husband orders.

"I don't believe it," Brianna breathed. "She said your salad was good."

"It was." He grinned. "I like those flavors together."

"Yes, but—" Brianna blinked.

Zac realized her eyes were full of tears.

"You're crying," he murmured, catching one tear on his fingertip. He slid his hand around her waist to comfort her. "Why?"

"Happy tears." She stared straight into his eyes. "I've never had a Thanksgiving like this before. Thank you."

"Me? I only made the salad," he said, loving the way she snuggled into him as if she found comfort in his arms.

"It was a great salad," she whispered as one hand brushed his jaw. "You're a great friend." Her eyes met his, huge orbs of forest green. "Thank you." Then Brianna stood on tiptoe and kissed him.

And Zac kissed her back, relishing the feel of her soft

lips against his, the touch of her fingers against his neck, the curve of her waist against his hand. She fit. This was right.

A noise from the doorway disturbed them but when he looked, no one was there and the discussion from the kitchen centered on whether knives should be points up or points down in the dishwasher.

Slightly bemused, Zac eased back a fraction so he could look into the face of the woman he loved, had never stopped loving.

"Brianna?"

"Yes?" She laid her head on his chest.

"Can we do this again sometime when we're alone?"

She froze for an instant, then giggled and drew out of his arms.

"That was the wrong thing to say, wasn't it?" he asked, hating the emptiness he felt at her loss. "I seem to make a habit of saying the wrong thing."

"On the contrary, my dear friend. You always say exactly the right thing to me." And she kissed him again, though this time her peck on his cheek was much less satisfying. "Let's get out the Christmas decorations. I have a feeling this is going to be an afternoon to remember."

Brianna didn't realize, but it already was, Zac thought, following her to the family room where a live tree waited to be adorned.

But where was it going? Did Brianna really care for him or was she just being a friend, as he'd asked? Or worse, was this whole day, the kiss, the embrace, simply because she felt sorry for him?

And why did it matter so much?

Because, Zac admitted to himself, he was head over heels in love with Brianna Benson.

Again.

Still.

* * *

Brianna stared at her mother, shocked by the hearty laughter from the woman who'd always seemed so full of anger.

"You can't hang those ornaments like that," she told Zac. "It looks ridiculous."

"It does look a little goofy," Cory agreed.

"Brianna?" Zac asked, drawing her out of her introspection.

"What?" She tore her gaze from her mother to study Zac's work. "Oh, definitely goofy. Some might even say weird."

"I would." Mr. Benson shrugged. "I'd like to support you, Zac, but sideways ornaments are too much for me."

The family looked at each other and burst into laughter. At him.

Brianna realized that for first time she could remember Zac seemed unbothered by that.

"Everybody's a critic," he mumbled as he righted the ornaments. "No vision."

"That was more like a nightmare." Brianna smiled and patted his cheek as she walked by. "But you have great vision in other areas."

"They're going to start talking about the church now," Cory warned.

"What about the church?" Mrs. Benson glared at him. "Are you changing things in our beautiful old church, too?"

"I don't know." Zac was always honest.

Brianna held her breath. This had been such an awesome day. She didn't want it ruined. But then, this was Zac. He knew how to handle her mother.

"Your daughter has a couple of clients who aspire to get into the construction trade. She thinks they should help with restoration at the church and she wants your husband to teach them."

"Hugh? You never told me this." Mrs. Benson frowned at her husband.

"Because I've decided not to do it. It takes away too much time I want to spend with you." He smiled as he covered her hand with his.

"But I won't be able to spend that much time talking to you. Brianna's got a quilt framed in my old office. I thought I'd come over and help her stitch it for a few hours a week." She looked at Brianna hesitantly. "If that would be all right?"

"Of course, Mom," Brianna said, her voice sounding wooden even to her. "If you want to help, I'd love it." However she knew her mother would criticize her efforts on the quilt she was making for Zac for Christmas.

"I think I would like to help." The older woman looked at her hands, flexed them. "Of course, there's no guarantee I can do it," she said, meeting Brianna's gaze. "If I make a mess of the stitches, I'll stop immediately. I wouldn't want to wreck your work."

"You wouldn't make a mess, Mom." For the first time in years, Brianna felt a connection with the woman who'd made her life so miserable. She knelt at her mother's side and slid her hands over her mother's weakened fingers. "A quilt is special because it's sewn with love," she whispered. "Not because of the stitches."

Her mother said nothing. She didn't have to. The harsh critical lines in her face softened. A tiny smile flickered at the corners of her mouth, then grew as she glanced around the room. Her gaze moved back to Brianna.

"Thank you," she whispered.

"Happy Thanksgiving, Mom."

As she hugged her mother, Brianna realized that her father's prayer had been answered. There was a spirit of peace and thanksgiving pervading this house.

And love.

If only Zac could be a permanent part of that. But he had other plans. He'd be leaving when he got that state job. Even if he could love her again, a future with him was impossible.

Because Brianna couldn't leave. Especially not now that she'd forged the first fragile bonds of reconciliation with her mother. Duty lay here in Hope. Duty to Cory, to her parents, to her clients. She'd run away once, but she couldn't do it a second time.

Zac would move on, but she'd given up her chance ten years ago. The realization decimated her but Brianna tried not to show anything as she drew away from her mother.

"Now, how about that pie?" she said, and hurried to the kitchen so she could dash away her tears before anyone saw them.

Chapter Thirteen

On Friday evening, Zac collapsed on his chaise longue.

"Don't you answer the door anymore?" Kent demanded a few minutes later as he towered over Zac, glaring.

"Didn't—hear—it." That was all Zac could manage as he sucked air into his starving lungs.

"Jogging." Kent's disgusted glare took in his clothes, soaked with sweat. "You're overdoing it, professor."

"Yeah."

"Why?"

The truth was too stupid to say aloud. Zac had run past Brianna's home umpteen times in hopes of seeing her, maybe getting invited in for coffee. He hadn't caught even a glimpse of her, but no way was he admitting that, so he grabbed his water bottle and drank in lieu of an answer.

"Never mind." Kent flopped down on another lounger. "I can't stay long. Jaclyn's tying up some odds and ends at the hospital. I have to pick her up in a few minutes. The reason I stopped by here is to tell you to get your sorry butt over to the church and help Brianna."

"Help her do what?" Zac raised one eyebrow.

"Cory has been regaling Brianna with her mother's tales of the church's past glory at Christmas, so for his sake, Brianna is trying to re-create it." Kent made a face. "I hid the ladders before I left and made her promise not to climb on anything, but you need to get over there or she's going to do herself an injury trying to satisfy that kid of hers."

"Where's Cory?" Zac's lungs began to lose the burning sensation.

"Working on his 'project' with his friends." Kent frowned. "What is this project, anyway?"

"I don't know," Zac admitted. "During Thanksgiving dinner he finally persuaded me to help his travel club plan a trip to Hawaii at Easter, so I don't think it's that."

"You had Thanksgiving at Brianna's?" Kent's blue eyes darkened at Zac's nod. "I see."

"You don't see anything," Zac said, rising. "It was nice. We decorated their tree. Her mother and Brianna made up. Sort of."

"And you and Brianna?" Kent said, raising one eyebrow. "Did you make up, too?"

"In a way. But it's not what you think." Sadness almost swamped him as he said it.

"Do you love her?"

The soft-voiced question halted Zac's progress inside. He stopped, turned around and sat down as he faced the truth.

"Yes," he admitted quietly. "But it isn't enough. I'm not enough."

"This again." Kent rolled his eyes.

"It's always been this," Zac told him. "Ever since she walked away. You know my goal. I want that job in curriculum. Kent, my past with Brianna is over."

"Who's talking about the past? I'm talking about the future. A future you and Brianna could have together." Kent hissed his frustration. "What's really at the bottom of this, Zac? If you love her—"

"Yes, I love Brianna. Always have. Okay?" Zac jumped

to his feet. "But so what? That doesn't make me any better suited to being her husband."

"What else do you need but love?" Kent demanded.

"This town, Hope, is your home and you think it's perfect," Zac muttered. "But it isn't perfect for me. I only came back here to take the next step on my journey."

"So you'll let your ambition ruin your relationship with Brianna again?" Kent's disgust was obvious.

"We're friends. We'll stay friends. But that's all," Zac told Kent. "Anyway what she does or doesn't feel for me isn't relevant."

"Isn't relevant?" Kent repeated.

"No, because whatever she feels, nothing can come of it." Zac watched Kent's eyes narrow and knew he had only a few minutes to make his point before his buddy would interrupt. "I've worked my entire life to get to the top, to prove that I'm not some useless brainy nerd. I've worked especially hard to prove it to the people in this town, the ones who made fun of me."

"You'll ignore what you feel for Brianna because you need revenge?" Kent demanded.

"No, but Brianna and I are on different paths now. I can't act on anything I feel because I'm not staying in Hope, Kent. Coming here was just a stepping stone onto something better. I need that state job."

"To prove you're not the poor pathetic nerd the kids in school called you?"

"Something like that." Zac stiffened at the reminder, the old scar stinging. "Brianna is not leaving Hope. She has her family, Cory has found his grandparents. She's finally working in the clinic she and her friends talked about half their life. It can't work between us."

"So you've decided, huh? Did you even pray about this?" Kent studied him then nodded. "I didn't think so. There's no room in your life for God to work, is there? Because Zac Ender already has his life all figured out, complete with barriers that no one can get through." Kent's voice hardened. "This need to prove yourself—it's a trap, Zac. And getting that state job won't satisfy you, because inside you won't have changed. You won't engage with those state administrators anymore than you did here because you're too afraid of rejection. But you can't control everything, Zac. Sometimes you just have to take a chance and trust God to work things out."

"Giving up control isn't that easy for me."

"I know." Kent nodded. "Because fear rules your life. You go out of your way to make sure nobody will reject you ever again, especially Brianna. You'll withdraw rather than extend yourself and take a chance. But the thing is, to find acceptance you have to be willing to risk rejection."

Zac recalled three occasions when he'd pled work as an excuse not to join his friends. He could have taken an hour off to join them but he hadn't, because he'd felt awkward.

"You've got your eyes focused on yourself, Zac. You talk about killing the apathy in the schools, about opening the kids' eyes, but yours are closed. You push people away, and then wonder why you're alone. I've known you most of my life and even I have to push my way into your world." Kent walked toward the gate, dragged it open then stopped to glare at him. "Fortunately for you, I happen to think you're worth the trouble."

"Thank you." Zac met his friend's blue stare with a nod.

"You're welcome. Now get over and help Brianna. I don't want her hobbling around with a cast for Christmas because you weren't man enough to get out of your comfort zone." Kent slapped on his cowboy hat. "Maybe you might even get to telling her how you really feel?"

"What good will that do?"

"Did you hear anything I said?" Kent shook his head in disgust. "You won't know till you try, will you?" He left.

Zac showered and changed in record time then drove to the church. He didn't have to. It wasn't far to walk. But he needed to talk to Brianna. When he arrived, she was kneeling in front of the manger scene at the side of the church, tenderly straightening the sheet that draped the baby doll.

She was sobbing.

"Hey!" Zac drew her to her feet and inspected her face. "What happened? Did you hurt yourself? Where?" He drew back to check.

"I'm f-fine. Oh, Zac." She shifted, pressed her face into his shoulder and began sobbing all over again.

Zac couldn't help but wrap his arms around her and try to comfort her. Finally her weeping slowed. She hiccupped once, drew away and swiped a hand across her face.

"What happened?" he asked, smoothing the damp strands away from her face.

"I'm an idiot, is what." Brianna sniffed, accepted the tissue he offered and blew her nose. "I'm so busy trying to impress my son that I slipped off a chair and singlehandedly destroyed the ornaments that are supposed to go on the Christmas tree. Precious old things and I ruined them all." Her face crumpled and tears began rolling down her cheeks again. "My mother will be furious when she finds out. She donated them."

"Don't start crying again, please?" he begged. Her tears made Zac feel helpless and awkward and useless. "Besides, they weren't just old, they were mostly chipped and broken. And worse than that, they were ugly. People should thank you. I wish I'd done it. It's the kind of thing I'm really good at."

"Oh, Zac." Brianna choked back a laugh.

"You can't defend those ugly baubles," he insisted, relieved to hear that laugh. "They were awful and should have been tossed years ago."

"Well, they were sort of ugly but—"

"No buts. I'm voting we start a new tradition." Zac wanted to hold her forever. Who cared that cars were driving slowly by, their inhabitants craning their neck to see who was embracing in front of the nativity display? With his arms wrapped around Brianna Benson he was in another world.

A world that couldn't last, his brain reminded.

"A new tradition? Such as?" She blinked at him, her lashes spiky from her weeping.

"Wait here. Okay? I'll be right back." He waited for her nod, tucked one wayward strand behind her ear then turned and ran toward his car. Less than five minutes later he was back with two large boxes. "Can you help me carry these inside? And don't you dare drop them."

"I'm not a klutz," Brianna replied with an inkling of her usual spirit. "What are they?"

"Remember the day we went to the Christmas farm? I made a purchase. Turned out to be a lot bigger than I realized."

He opened the boxes and lifted out the beautiful blown glass balls he'd purchased.

"Oh." Brianna clasped her hands to her cheeks, green eyes flaring with excitement. "I love these. But don't you want to use them at home?"

"I did." Zac smiled at her rapt expression. "These are what are left. Turns out I ordered a dozen of each, instead of one. When that clerk said the price I thought they sounded awfully expensive but then Cory said you loved them so I figured to heck with the expense. If Brianna—" He stopped, aware that he'd just given himself away.

"You bought them because you thought I liked them?" Brianna's eyes grew even more round. "Really?"

Be open, Kent had charged him. *Meet the other person halfway.*

"Yes."

"Oh, Zac. I've prayed and prayed—" She put a hand over her mouth.

"You've prayed for me?" he asked, and knew from her expression that it was true. "I've prayed for you, too. For you and Cory and your parents." He slid his hand over hers. "I want you to be happy."

"I'm very happy right now," Brianna whispered, and tilted just the slightest bit forward.

Zac wasn't stupid. He knew there was no future for them, but this was an opportunity he wasn't going to resist. He drew her into his arms and kissed her. Her lips were soft and inviting beneath his and after a second she freed her hands to wrap them around him and drew him closer. It was as if ten years had never passed.

This was right, his brain chirped as he deepened the embrace, pouring feelings he couldn't verbalize in his caress. This was what should be. But just as Zac tried to draw Brianna even closer, she pushed back, tilting her head away from him.

"What are we doing, Zac?" she whispered.

"Kissing." He grinned at her. "Didn't you like it?"

He thought she'd joke back. But her eyes darkened to a rich forest-green as she stared at him.

"I always did like kissing you," she murmured. "You make me feel like I matter. When I'm in your arms I feel protected, as if I don't have to be the strong one anymore."

"You don't," Zac told her, a rush of confidence filling him.

"For how long?" Brianna broke eye contact then eased

away from him. In one fluid motion she slipped out of his arms. With a delicate touch she slid a wire hanger through the glistening glass balls then balanced on tiptoe as she hung them all over the tree. "Sooner or later you'll be leaving, Zac," she whispered.

And there it was—the stark, cold truth. There was nothing he could say to contradict her. So he worked silently alongside her, placing the ornaments on the higher branches she couldn't reach.

"Did you mean what you said?" Brianna asked sometime later.

"I always mean what I say." He fastened the last ball, then straightened. "But which time, exactly?"

"A few weeks ago you told me that back then, when we were supposed to be getting married, you would have given up your dream for me. Was that true, Zac?"

Zac took a minute to plug in the Christmas-tree lights and admire the soft shimmer of their beauty reflected in the beautiful ornaments. He needed the time to choose his words wisely because he must not hurt her.

"I probably would have, Brianna."

"But you would have regretted it." She looked deflated, as if all hope had drained out of her. "I see." She turned away but he caught her arm, urged her to look at him.

"I've learned some things about myself since then," he said.

"Such as?"

Okay. Kent told him to open up. Here it was.

"I need to be validated, Brianna," he told her. "Somewhere inside me there's a little kid demanding I show all the people who once laughed at me."

"Show them what?" Brianna's smooth forehead rumpled.

"That I'm worth their respect. That I'm not a nerd. That I've done a lot with my life." Zac waited for it, but Brianna wasn't laughing at him. With a sweet rush of feeling he realized that she never had. So he continued to tell her what was in his heart. "That's why I said it's a good thing we didn't get married. I couldn't stay in Hope. I needed to prove myself."

"But, Zac." She stopped, frowned and then waved a hand. "Look around. Who is there to show? Everyone has moved on with their lives. They're not noticing you or what you've accomplished. You're not in high school anymore."

The way she said it made him feel like a child.

"Why did you kiss me, Zac?" Brianna demanded. "Because I was here and handy? Because you were trying to comfort me?"

"Because you were sad, and I wanted to make you feel better. Because I care about you, Brianna." That was about as open as Zac could get. He looked at her but she seemed to be waiting for him to continue. "I like kissing you."

"I like kissing you, too." A soft smile creased her lips. "But is that all there is?"

"It has to be," he said softly.

"Because?"

"Because you're staying here in Hope, and I'm leaving, Brianna. Maybe not today or tomorrow, but as soon as I can." Zac squeezed her forearms then let go and took a step backward. "I wish I could offer you a future. I wish we could build on what we've learned about each other, but it wouldn't be fair to you because I won't be staying and you can't go."

"No, I can't." She wrapped her arms around herself as if seeking comfort. "Mom and I have some kind of truce started. I have to see that through. And Cory would never forgive me if I took him away from his grandparents now."

"I know." Zac reached out and brushed the curling tendril away from her eyes. "I know it's stupid, Brianna. This need I have to prove myself—I know it's childish, that nobody cares. But I care. I need to show the world—"

"What?" she whispered when he didn't continue.

That I'm worth loving.

The unspoken words shocked him. Zac stared at Brianna, realizing that the hole in his heart that had opened up the day she left still gaped.

And that when he left Hope, it was never going to heal.

"I think that if you try a few of those suggestions, you'll find it a lot easier to get along with your family this Christmas." Brianna smiled at her troubled student and escorted her to her office door. "Let me know how it turns out."

"I will. Thanks." She gathered up her coat. "I have to hurry. The Your World fair starts in an hour. Merry Christmas, Ms. Benson."

"Yes, Merry Christmas to you, Trina." Brianna sank down behind her desk only after the girl had left.

The Your World fair.

For the past three weeks she'd worked alongside Zac, preparing for today while her heart cracked and broke. Not once in all that time had he mentioned the night at the church, so neither had she. He'd escorted her home without saying anything and she'd taken her cue from his silence and kept it through every encounter.

Though his hand might brush hers, though she laughed and smiled, the approaching Christmas season left Brianna anything but happy. She missed their frank discussions, the comfort he offered whenever her mother lapsed back into her old habits. And she'd tried to explain to Cory why Zac no longer came over.

In the stillness of the night, after everyone had gone to bed, Brianna faced the certain knowledge that she loved Zac Ender with all of her heart, that she would love him until the day she died. Zac made her world sparkle and shine. Without him the day passed slowly. But Zac was leaving. And she had to stay. Her father's health had deteriorated. Her mother was not recovering from her stroke as quickly as expected. Cory had abandoned his self-destructive behavior but to uproot him now was a chance Brianna dare not take. Her place was here.

Zac's was not.

To keep facing him day after day when all she wanted was to throw herself in his arms and beg him to stay was torture. Everything reminded her of him—the apple pie she'd made last week was his favorite. The manger scene she'd set on a window ledge was one he'd given her eons ago. The green dress she wore today—it reminded her how he'd once admired a green outfit because he said it made her eyes mysterious. But that night at the church, when he'd held her so tenderly, then told her he would be leaving, that's when she'd known her love would never be returned.

"Oh, Lord, this is so hard." She squeezed her eyes against the tears. "But You are my comfort. You know how my heart hurts. You know my deepest desires and You will guide me on the best route for my life, even if it's without Zac." As she'd done for the past few months, she repeated, "Use me however You want, God. Let me be a living testament to You. Help me show Your love to others."

Thus strengthened and resting in the knowledge that God would always be there for her, she gathered her jacket and her purse and headed for the school, smiling at everyone she passed.

This would be the most difficult Christmas she'd ever spent.

"Hey, Mr. E. Pretty amazing, isn't it?" The student grinned at Zac's openmouthed gape. "We pulled out all the stops."

"You sure did." Zac had already noticed the huge banner outside announcing the Your World fair. In the foyer were directive signs leading to the auditorium but it was inside that auditorium that brought surprise.

The room was divided into booths with signs hanging over each one announcing the student's goal or dream. Charts, models, illustrations—each booth featured some practical application of their point. Students had grouped together in some cases, or gone it alone in others. The room brimmed with Christmas decorations, all handmade by the students. The total effect was amazing.

"Mr. Ender, we've kept folks waiting, hoping you'd do us the honor of saying a little something to open our Your World fair." The principal smiled at him. "Would you mind?"

"I'd be happy to." The words slipped out without thought. Then Zac caught sight of the press of people waiting outside the gym doors. He followed the principal to the small podium and took his place on it, heart in his mouth as he scanned their faces. His throat went dry. His palms began to sweat. What should he say?

He saw Brianna, standing at the rear of the group. Her eyes met his. She smiled at him and suddenly Zac felt calmer.

"Ms. Benson has been my cohort in helping create Your World," he told the principal. "I think she should be up here, too."

The principal agreed and sent a student to lead her forward. She stood beside him, leaned closer and said, "Congratulations, Zac. But who invited all these people to our little soiree?"

"I have no idea." He looked at her and saw a flicker of sadness in her eyes, which she quickly concealed. "I'm going to try to make an off-the-cuff speech to open this thing," he murmured. "When I screw up, bail me out."

"You won't screw up. Just speak from your heart."

Zac got lost in her eyes. Why did she always have such confidence in him?

"Ladies and gentlemen, today we are going to w-witness our future, as seen by your children. You may consider their ideas mere flights of fancy. You may think their goals impossible." Zac stopped, his throat desert dry from nervousness. The room was so quiet.

Brianna stepped forward.

"We ask you to suspend those thoughts and let yourself fully experience the hopes and dreams of the young people of this community," she continued. "Examine them. Talk about them. Learn how our world looks to those who will inherit it." She laid her hand over Zac's, which held a huge pair of scissors. "So now, on behalf of the students of Hope schools—" She looked at Zac, waited.

A rush of confidence filled him. He could do this—with her.

"We hereby declare Hope's Your World fair open." He and Brianna cut the ribbon.

There was much applause then people began to stream inside.

"Thank you," Zac said to her. "I'm glad you rescued me."

"You didn't need rescuing," Brianna said. "You were speaking from your heart. People respect that."

A man stepped in front of them, identified himself as media from Las Cruces and asked many questions. When he left there was another, and another.

"How did you hear about this?" Zac finally asked.

"Press release. Want to see it?" The reporter pulled a crumpled piece of paper from his shirt pocket and handed it over. "Smart way to drum up interest," he said.

Zac smoothed the paper and studied it, conscious of Brianna leaning over one shoulder.

"Wait a minute. I recognize this." She took it from him, squinted at the artwork. "Cory did this."

"Cory? Are you sure?" But the more Zac studied the paper, the more he realized the phrasings were not those of an adult. "Your son drummed up all this interest," he said, waving a hand as locals and strangers alike filed into the auditorium. He looked at Brianna. "You're not crying, are you?" he asked.

"Tears of pride," she assured him with a teary smile.

"Well, you'd better wipe them away," he said tenderly as he dabbed at her face with his handkerchief. "You'll embarrass him."

Brianna laughed. And then her eyes locked with his and all Zac wanted to do was pull her close and hold her. Of its own volition, his hand reached out. His fingers grazed her sleeve but a voice stopped him.

"Excuse me? Are you Zachary Ender?"

"Yes," he replied.

Two men introduced themselves and gave their credentials from state education.

"We were told of this plan of yours and were intrigued. It certainly seems to have interested the kids and the town." The men explained that a letter from a student inviting them to the event had arrived at their office two days earlier. "Anyone who can generate student interest as you have certainly bears our closer inspection. Would you show us around?"

Zac wanted Brianna to come along but she excused herself. So he ushered the men inside and began telling them how Your World had started. Over the next couple of hours he caught sight of Brianna. Once she was laughing with Eve Larsen. But twice she stood in one corner, a serious expression marring her beauty as she listened to a red-faced parent.

Zac wanted to go to her, but he could not leave the state people. He could not abandon this chance to make his mark on them, to prove himself.

Brianna had been a mediator, he reminded himself. She would handle the parents with aplomb. But as the day progressed, a niggling worry kept him glancing around the room to find her.

"Is something wrong?" one of the men asked.

"Not at all." Zac abandoned his current search of the room. "Let's have lunch. The students' travel club is raising funds for a trip to Hawaii. They're selling soup and sandwiches."

Brianna would manage without him.

"Hi, Mom."

"Cory!" She hugged him then his two friends. "You guys and your secrets. You're the PR behind this event, aren't you?"

"Yeah." Cory grinned as he high-fived his buddies. "Adam's thinking about a career as a sports agent, and Hart's into newspaper stuff so we put our heads together."

"You did a marvelous job," she told them. "I'm so proud of all three of you."

"Thanks." Cory showed her some leaflets. "We're passing these out in case anybody here wants to hire us. Then we'll be able to raise more money for the travel club."

"Get busy then," she said. "I'll buy your lunch when you're ready." They hurried away, chatting between themselves as they spread their leaflets.

Brianna spent a few moments surveying the room decorated in red, white and green—and its very engaged students. Zac had done an amazing job in the school, and she felt a surge of pride and rich satisfaction in having been part of his goal to turn around the town's young people.

That combined with the change he'd wrought in Cory had helped her face her anger at God so that she now realized He was there with her even though she didn't feel Him. She'd gained a new relationship with her father and her mother, thanks to Zac. He'd helped her cleanse the failures of the past.

But not even Zac could erase the failure she felt in her work.

Brianna had tried so hard to help kids, to ensure that they had someone there to listen to them. But it seemed all she'd done was create barriers between parents and the children whose aspirations they couldn't accept.

"I want to talk to you," Peter Larsen said, standing in front of her, his face belligerent.

"Let's get out of the way where we can talk more freely." Brianna's heart sank as she led him to a quiet spot behind the stage. "What's on your mind, Peter?"

"I like to be honest and up front so I'm telling this to your face. We're circulating a petition to have the school board remove student-counseling services from Whispering Hope Clinic."

"Because of Your World?" she asked, trying to stem the pain at this new evidence of her failure. "But I thought that once you saw what the students are learning—"

"Because of you." His jaw thrust forward. "We don't want our kids to waste their lives dreaming of something they'll never have. You've got my Eve out there, her head in the clouds as she talks to those state people about going to medical school. We both know she isn't smart enough. It's not going to happen."

"But it can—"

"You think running away from this place solves everything. I don't want my kid running away, trying to achieve something she can't get. I know all about that." Peter clamped his lips together, as if he'd said too much.

"Is that what this is about?" Brianna murmured, stunned by his words. "Is what's bothering you the fact that you didn't get your dreams, and you don't want Eve to experience the disappointment you did?"

"Yes." His anger flared. "I found nothing but pain when I left this place. I thought I could make something of myself but all I managed was to get caught up in drugs because then I didn't have to feel the disappointment."

"There's no guarantee Eve will go through that," she told him, feeling his pain.

"There's no guarantee she won't. I came really close to killing myself once," he admitted in a very soft voice. "I will not lose my baby girl."

"But that's what you're risking by not sharing her dream and helping her find a way to achieve it."

For a second Brianna thought he'd recant, but then laughter from the other room intruded and his face hardened.

"I just wanted to warn you," he said. "We're going to talk to the school board after this thing is over. We don't want you around our kids anymore."

Brianna watched him stomp away. She heard someone approaching. Quickly she moved to stand behind the stage drapes, hidden as tears of bitterness rolled down her cheeks.

"This has been an amazing display, Zac," one of the state men said. "You've taken the worst of the schools in this area and turned it around. We wanted to let you know that if you're interested, we have room for you in our office. Whenever you like."

"Thank you very much. I'd enjoy the chance to enhance curriculum."

Brianna tuned out the rest of the conversation, didn't

even notice when they left. All she could think about was that Zac had achieved his goal.

And she had failed to reach hers.

Her heart was glad for him. He'd worked so hard. He deserved every success.

She loved him, but it was futile.

Zac would leave Hope. Brianna couldn't.

She finally accepted that they had no future together.

Chapter Fourteen

Zac returned to the auditorium elated that as he'd escorted the state men to their vehicle, they'd assured him he'd have a job offer on his desk in the New Year.

Jubilant that he'd finally achieved his goal, he couldn't wait to find Brianna and share the news with her. Then he realized that after he left, he wouldn't be able to share anything with her ever again. The realization knocked him for a loop.

Brianna would be out of his life forever.

Was that what he wanted?

"We have to talk to you, Zac." Peter Larsen stood in front of him, his face set in angry lines. Behind him several other parents were nodding.

Aware that the confrontation was causing a disturbance in the room, and embarrassed that they were now the center of attention, that he was being targeted this way, Zac needed to get them out of here.

"Uh, sure." Zac glanced around. "Let's go somewhere more private."

"We can talk right here. Other parents need to hear this." Pete glared at him.

Trepidation crawled up Zac's spine and took root like a

hammer in his head. Everyone was staring. He was caught like a deer in the spotlights with the entire room looking on, the center of attention—the very last thing he wanted.

"I've already told Brianna that we're going to ask the school board to cancel the contract for counseling with Whispering Hope Clinic."

"What?" Zac blinked. Peter's face was white. An angry line creased his forehead. "You'd do that—after what you've seen here today?" he asked, keeping his voice low, moderated.

"This fair doesn't change anything. In fact, it makes it worse," Peter sputtered. "Now other people have latched on to the fairy tale and that's wrong. We all know nothing's going to change. Somebody has to deal with reality here in Hope. So I'll be the bad guy. We don't want Brianna filling our kids' heads with silly impossible dreams anymore. It's too hard on us parents when we can't make them come true."

"Too hard on you?" Fury banished any trace of awkwardness Zac felt at being on display. That the Larsens and other parents would do this to the caring woman who'd tried so hard to help them and their families infuriated him. Every single eye in the gym was on him, but Zac was barely conscious of the audience. He looked Peter straight in the eye.

"Have you lost your memory?" he demanded. "Can't you remember four months ago when your little girl made a desperate attempt to escape the misery of her life here in Hope because she had no goals, no dreams?"

The other man paled, but Zac couldn't stop. They'd impugned the integrity of a woman who'd gone way beyond anything in her job description to help their children. He could not sit back and allow that.

"You think dreaming about a career as a doctor is harmful to Eve because you can't make it come true? Why is it up to you? It's Eve's dream." He faced the next man. "And you, Martin? You think your son's aspiration to get into the space program is silly? And Grant? You don't want that brilliant kid of yours to go into cancer research? Why? Why would any of you want to kill such laudable goals as these?"

The group squirmed but they didn't back down.

"They're impossible goals," Grant mumbled.

"Who says they are?" Zac shook his head. "Four months ago your kids aspired to nothing. They were failing in school, destined to fail in life because nobody gave them hope and nobody told them they could have a dream and achieve it. You, their parents, had failed them and you know it. Yet not one single one of you came running to me, asking me to help you change things. You were content to let them share your apathy."

"We were not apathetic about our kids!" Martin was red-faced now. "We wanted better for them."

"Just not the better they want, is that it?" Zac shook his head. "I think you've let yourselves get so bowed down by your own unfulfilled dreams, you believed your kids didn't have what it took to change the status quo. And when they challenged that, you reacted by letting fear control you." Zac paused. If he was going to connect with these angry parents, he was going to have to be brutally honest. "The reason I believe that is because I was in the same position, believing a lie because I feared the truth."

Zac let the images of the past four months flood his mind, the certainty that he had to leave here to be successful, the conviction that he had to escape teaching and the spotlight to make a difference.

"I was just like you, caught up in escaping my own failures, certain I could change nothing—until Brianna pushed into our lives. She's challenged us, you, your kids and me, to look beyond our safe little world and see what is around us. She defies our rigid mind-sets and dares us to be better than we are, to look beyond Hope to the world and imagine how we can affect it. To feel our fear, acknowledge it and push past it."

The room remained utterly silent. Zac knew he was the focus but it didn't matter. What mattered was making these parents see the truth.

"Yes, Brianna and I helped your kids begin to dream, Peter. We asked them to see themselves in a world where their contributions matter. And this—" he waved a hand "—this is the amazing answer your kids gave."

"But it's just a dream," Grant protested.

"What's wrong with that? Didn't space travel, the United Nations, the internet all start with a dream? The how and why of it came later." Zac let his emotions run free as he studied the other men, then moved his arm to indicate the various displays. "This is your chance for success, Peter. And yours, Martin. And Grant's. In this room lies the best chance we in Hope have to impact the world around us by equipping our kids with our wholehearted support for whatever they dream, by not being afraid, by embracing it, by pushing them toward it."

Zac slung an arm around Peter's shoulders, the man who as a teen had berated him so often. For Zac that past was gone. The hurt was over. The need to prove himself had been replaced by the need to help the kids.

"Your businesses in Hope are important, of course, but your real legacy lies in your kids, great kids who want to change the world whether they decide to stay here in town or whether they want to move away. But their success hinges on you and me getting rid of our fear." He decided to take a risk. "Think about how different your world and mine would have been if we'd had a counselor like Brianna when we were in school, someone who told us to believe in ourselves, someone who pushed us beyond our fears to our dreams."

"But how can they do it?" Peter demanded. "It's impossible."

"That's fear talking. Fear of failure. It's what a lot of people said about going to the moon." Zac stepped away, shook his head. "And if you think like that, you're already defeated. That's why we need Brianna. She doesn't say it will be easy or fast or any of that. All she's saying is try. If it weren't for her selflessness, her vision, her foresight and most of all her courage and determination, you parents would have little to feel proud of today. But because of her, your kids' futures are wide open for whatever they aspire to. All they have to do is reach."

Zac glanced around and realized he wasn't a bit nervous. He loved Brianna, loved her more than anything. He would do whatever it took to defend her. It had never been that God couldn't use him. It had been his fear that prevented God's work. No more.

He stared at the assembly, let the silence stretch until every eye in the place was on him.

"How sad that you're rejecting the one person who's put hope back in Hope. But if that's truly the way you feel, I'm tendering my resignation. Effective immediately."

A collective gasp went up.

"No. We don't want that. You've done a great job for us, Zac." Martin shook his head. "I'm not willing to go along with you on this anymore, Peter. My kids have done a one-eighty in school. I didn't like hearing their grandiose plans because it made me feel a failure and because I was afraid they were doomed to the same. But my mess isn't theirs."

"But you don't—"

"No, I don't know how we're going to pay for my son to go to college, but he's going, Peter. He's going as an emissary of Hope into a world where he's needed." Martin's shoulders went back and his chin lifted. "I say we keep Brianna doing what she's doing. I didn't trust my kids enough to believe in them, or her. I've been walking around in fear, but that ends now."

"I agree," Grant said, his voice quieter. "My mom died of cancer. Imagine if my kid found a cure. What a legacy. I don't know how we'll manage. I have no money to send him to college. But if my boy wants to go, I'm sending him. There's got to be a way."

One by one other parents in the group murmured their assent. Somehow Peter seemed to sink back into the crowd as Kent stepped forward.

"I say we owe Zac a big round of applause. When my kid goes to this school, he's going to benefit from all the work Zac's done."

Zac cut short the clapping. "I think your thanks should be to Brianna."

Everyone cheered and called her name. Zac worried she'd run away until finally Brianna appeared from behind the corner of a stage drape. She looked stunned by the attention and accolades as she moved to the stairs. Zac walked forward and held out a hand to help her dismount.

"Three cheers for Brianna. Hip, hip, hooray!" the crowd shouted with their approval.

Zac had never been more proud.

Or more certain of what he had to do to prove himself to her and finally be free.

Brianna gulped down her tears as Cory's two friends stepped forward with a sheaf of roses. She hugged them both, then tried to think of what to say to express what was in her heart.

"Thank you. Thank you all. I know I've tried your patience." She smiled as the room erupted into laughter. "But I believe, as Zac does, in our kids. They are our future. They are so much smarter than we were. They see the world as their responsibility and they are determined to make a positive impact on it. I applaud you, students. Congratulations." She shifted her roses and clapped for them. The parents joined her.

The kids in the room laughed and bowed, their faces beaming when their parents rushed over for a hug.

Awed by the response and that her prayer to be able to help kids had been so completely answered, Brianna tried to slip away, but Zac prevented that by taking her hand. She studied his face, amazed at the transformative glow that softened the angles and edges.

"Thank you," she said and tried to lift her hand free. But Zac wouldn't let go.

"I'm not finished, Brianna. I have something else to say," he said more loudly, drawing the attention of the room. Every eye turned on them.

Brianna shifted uncomfortably, wishing she knew why Zac had done this. It was so unlike him to draw attention to himself.

"Bear with me now, folks. Everyone knows I'm the worst public speaker this town has ever seen." He paused to let the murmur of laughter subside. "I'm also the slowest learner. For years I thought that if I could make a big enough impact, I could show everyone that I'm not the nerdy failure I thought they saw when they looked at me. Then you came back to town, Brianna, and I had to face the fact that my true failure was that I was afraid to believe in us, even though I loved you. Even though I never stopped loving you."

Brianna gasped. She glanced around the room, quivering under the interested stares. Her knees began to shake. What was Zac doing?

"I've just stood here and criticized Peter for not taking a risk on his daughter, but that's exactly what I refused to do with us. I want a future with you but I was too afraid to tell you I loved you in case you turned me down or changed your mind. Again."

A soft whiff of laughter rolled around the room.

"Zac, this—"

"This is me, Brianna. Warts and all. And I am in love with you. Still. Forever." Zac knelt on one knee. "Brianna Benson, will you marry me?"

Chapter Fifteen

Zac waited, kneeling, holding her hand.

Brianna found not a trace of embarrassment on his face.

But how could she answer? If she said yes—well, he was leaving. And she couldn't leave.

But if she said no he'd be horribly embarrassed in a town where she'd already done that to him once.

"I've never known you to be at a loss for words, Brianna." Zac's eyes held hers, strong, determined and brimming with love. For her.

And then it dawned on her. She'd learned to trust God, even when she didn't feel Him. She believed He had been guiding her to reconciliation with her mother, to help Cory change, to her own healing. This second chance at love was her test, the biggest test of all. She could accept it and believe God would work out the details, as she'd told the students so many times, or she could run away again.

Brianna wasn't running anymore.

"Yes, I will marry you, Zac. Whenever you want. I love you."

In a flash she was in his arms and he was kissing her in front of the entire assembly, to the wild applause of students and parents. He finally drew away, but refused to release her.

"I hereby declare Your World fair over," he said in a clear firm voice, a grin stretching his mouth. "But you're welcome to stay for coffee and Christmas cookies. The travel club could use your support. Merry Christmas everyone."

"Merry Christmas," the group repeated as one and then to each other.

Brianna stood by Zac's side while the townspeople filed past them, congratulating them and offering to help with the wedding, which Zac claimed would be as soon as possible.

Cory was the last in line. He shook Zac's hand and welcomed him to the family. Then he hugged his mother tightly.

"I'm sorry I messed up so badly," he said for her ears alone. "I promise I'll try harder to make you proud, even if the judge thinks I should go to detention."

"I'm already very proud," she told him, kissing his cheek. "No matter what the judge decides. We'll keep praying until your video conference with him tomorrow."

"When he hears what you've done for the fair, I'm sure he'll be impressed," Zac said. "Besides, you have to be here for the wedding. Who else would be my best man?"

Cory left them to tell his friends, his chest three inches bigger.

"If you're free for the rest of the afternoon, I think we should go ring shopping." Zac leaned nearer and brushed her cheek with his lips. The auditorium had emptied. Everyone had gone. They were all alone.

"I already have a ring." Brianna drew the chain holding her ten-year-old engagement ring from beneath her sweater. "I love this ring. I don't need another."

"This ring is okay," Zac said, slipping it free of the chain. "But it needs a few alterations because we've gone through a few changes ourselves. For the better," he added. "I promise I'll give it back to you on Christmas Eve. And I don't expect you to wear it on a chain around your neck."

She giggled and agreed, but a moment later grew serious.

"I heard those men offer you the job, Zac. What are you going to do?" A whisker of fear tickled inside but Brianna forced it away. God would work it out. She knew that.

"I'm going to decline. I want to be here to find out what happens to our first Your World graduates," he told her, fiddling with the tendril that refused to lie against her neck. "I want to be here to watch you and your mom grow closer. I want to be here to help your dad take care of our family. Mostly I want to be with you and work with you to help kids excel."

"That's what I want, too, but only if you're sure. After all, that state job was your dream."

"My dreams have changed, Brianna, and all of them include you and me together, making a difference in children's lives. Today I finally realized that if I make myself available, God can use me." He made a self-deprecating gesture. "I could never have spoken that long to all those people except that I asked God to use me. From now on I'm available to Him. And you."

He kissed her and for a few moments they basked in their joy. But Brianna had to ask.

"Why did you choose such a public forum to propose?"

"Something your mom said last night when I saw her after visiting Miss Latimer. She said, 'If you want someone to know something, Zac, you have to tell them.' I decided I'd make sure you knew I loved you. Besides, after accepting me publicly, you can't really back out, can you?"

"I'm not backing out ever," she told him. "I'm trusting God. He always knows what's best. Let's go enjoy our Christmas break, fiancé."

* * *

The Christmas Eve service at the tiny run-down church was short but filled with meaning. As Brianna sat beside Zac listening to the age-old words announcing the birth of Christ, she marveled at what God had done for her.

The judge, so impressed with Cory's work and the reports from his teachers as well as a commendation from a news agency who had received his press release, had granted an unconditional discharge. Brianna spared a moment to think of Craig.

"We'll look after him, Craig. Zac and I will love your son as long as we live."

The root of betrayal that had lain dormant for so long was gone. Brianna was finally free to embrace her future with Zac.

When the service was over, Brianna watched her father wheel her mother out of the sanctuary. They looked like newlyweds themselves, beaming with happiness as Cory danced beside them, asking a ton of questions.

"Do you have to get home right away? Can we take a moment?" Zac whispered in her ear.

"We have all the time in the world." She smiled at him, content to stand beside him, her hand nestled in his, studying the lovely Christmas tree they'd decorated together.

Finally they were alone.

"This is for you." Zac slid a ring on her finger. But it wasn't her old ring. It was a completely different one. A lovely diamond solitaire that glittered above a circle of smaller diamonds that enclosed it and kept it safe. "I love you, Brianna."

He kissed her thoroughly, and of course Brianna responded.

"It's beautiful, Zac, and I love it," she told him when she

could catch her breath. "But what happened to the other diamond?"

"You'll see when I slide your wedding ring on your finger." He kissed the ring in place, then in the glow of the Christmas-tree lights lifted her face so he could look into her eyes. "I don't want to wait anymore, Brianna. Can we please get married New Year's Eve?"

"New Year's Eve? But it's so soon."

"Soon? I've waited ten years!" Zac grinned. "The whole town has offered to help us. And a client of yours, Trina, approached me today to offer her help. Seems she's planning a future as a wedding consultant and says she needs the practice."

Brianna burst out laughing. But then she looked at the man she loved, had loved, would love. The moment grew solemn. His eyes held hers, a plea in their dark depths.

"I would love to marry you on New Year's Eve, Zac." She stood on tiptoe and kissed him. "Just tell me the time, and I'll be there."

"You're sure?" he asked, staring deeply into her eyes.

"Positive."

After one last kiss, they left the church and drove home where they announced their news to friends and family who'd gathered there.

And when they'd all departed and no one but Brianna and Zac remained, he led her outside onto the deck and pointed to the black velvet sky, glittering with stars.

"This is our world. I can't guarantee we'll be here forever, but I can guarantee that for as long as God gives us, I will always love you," Zac murmured, holding her in the circle of his arms. "Forever."

"Forever," Brianna agreed. "That should be just about long enough for us to learn to love each other enough so we can trust each other with everything. She glanced upward. "A certain elf named Cory used up many allowances hanging this mistletoe all over the place."

"Did not," a voice denied. Then a window slammed closed.

Zac's chest shook with laughter. He drew Brianna even closer.

"By all means let's not waste the boy's allowance," he murmured.

He guessed that Brianna's heartfelt response meant she totally agreed.

* * * * *

Dear Reader,

Welcome back to Hope, New Mexico. I hope you enjoyed Brianna and Zac's story. They waited a long time and waded through a lot of issues before they finally gave love a second chance. Brianna had to deal with her unmet expectations of Zac, and he had to face his fear of letting folks see the real person he is.

I hope you'll join me for the third installment of this series, *Healing Hearts*, when the third couple join their friends in Hope. Shay Parker and Nick Green have no idea of how coming home is about to change their lives. Look for their story, *Perfectly Matched*, in March.

I love to hear from readers and will do my best to answer as quickly as possible. You can contact me at my webpage at www.loisricher.com; email me at loisricher@yahoo.com or like me on Facebook. Or you can write me at Box 639, Nipawin, Sask., Canada S0E 1E0.

Until we meet again, I wish you overflowing joy that Jesus brought, abundant love God reserves for each of us and a peace to pass on to those around you.

Merry Christmas and Happy New Year from my house to yours!

Blessings,

Lois
Richer

Questions for Discussion

1. Brianna thought she knew Zac very well, but the evening before their wedding she realized she was mistaken. Have you ever been negatively surprised by the actions of someone you thought you knew? Discuss your reaction and how this affected future encounters.

2. Zac thought he had a problem making public presentations but realized that his fear stemmed from something much deeper—an inability to trust. Examine ways trust issues force each of us to be less that honest sometimes.

3. Brianna's difficulty with her mother's domineering behavior affected their relationship so negatively that it became a huge barrier even after ten years. What counsel would you give today to a teenage Brianna to help her deal with her mother's attitude and actions?

4. Brianna felt a huge responsibility to keep her vow to her dead friend and return to work in the clinic in Hope. Talk about your motivations in regard to life changes you have made.

5. Zac was affected by not fitting in with the school crowd, of being the odd man out. As Christians we live in the world and interact with it every day. Are there ways you could help children and teens to retain their faith and their goals and yet still reach out to the students around them? How would you have helped Zac?

6. Zac was also affected by his experience with a student who died from a drug overdose. He drew his

life's goal from that experience and determined to help kids see the potential in their future. Discuss how we as parents, teachers, leaders and members of our communities can challenge kids to reach higher and further.

7. Brianna had a difficult time getting the parents of her clients to accept their children's goals, just as her mother never accepted hers. Share instances when you have given lip service to something but found it much harder to actually let go and not only allow but encouraged your child, your spouse or your friend to venture far beyond your expectations.

8. Zac made it a point to visit a former teacher in the nursing home. Consider ways you can be a blessing to someone who gave important years of their life to help you.

9. When Zac finally got the focus off of himself and poured out his heart without worrying about how he'd look, he impacted everyone. Discuss ways each of us is rendered less effective because we are too self-conscious.

10. For years Brianna pushed her way through life feeling abandoned by God. Zac thought he wasn't God material. Chat about ways we limit what God can do because we have a wrong view of Him.

11. Zac and Brianna both learned that God could handle their complaints and criticisms. Do you feel this is irreverent? How has the honesty of telling God how you really feel affected your relationship with Him?

12. At the end of the book, Zac gave up his dreams of curriculum work to stay in Hope with Brianna. Do you feel this sacrifice was too much to ask? How would you have advised him?

RANCHER'S REFUGE
Whisper Falls
Linda Goodnight
Both running from their pasts, Annalisa Keller and Austin Blackwell learn that painful secrets are washed away beneath Whisper Falls—where prayers actually are answered.

HOMECOMING REUNION
Home to Hartley Creek
Carolyne Aarsen
Garret Beck always thought money gave him control over life, but reconnecting with first love Larissa Weir makes him question what really matters.

FALLING FOR THE FOREST RANGER
Leigh Bale
The dangers of the untamed Idaho rivers drive Tanner Bohlman to protect Zoë Lawton and her son, even if the beautiful marine biologist has more grit than he gives her credit for!

DOCTOR TO THE RESCUE
Eagle Point Emergency
Cheryl Wyatt
When she agrees to babysit former combat doctor Ian Shupe's little girl, Bri Landis has her heart touched by father *and* daughter as both struggle to trust again.

SMALL-TOWN DAD
Jean C. Gordon
Wanting to recapture the life he lost while raising his daughter alone, Neil Hazard can't possibly let Anne Howard and her precious toddler into his future—can he?

A DAUGHTER'S REDEMPTION
Georgiana Daniels
Robyn Warner has unknowingly fallen for the cop responsible for her father's death...but Caleb Sloane just can't bring himself to walk away from the grieving woman.

REQUEST YOUR FREE BOOKS!

2 FREE INSPIRATIONAL NOVELS
PLUS 2
FREE
MYSTERY GIFTS

Love Inspired

YES! Please send me 2 FREE Love Inspired® novels and my 2 FREE mystery gifts (gifts are worth about $10). After receiving them, if I don't wish to receive any more books, I can return the shipping statement marked "cancel." If I don't cancel, I will receive 6 brand-new novels every month and be billed just $4.49 per book in the U.S. or $4.99 per book in Canada. That's a saving of at least 22% off the cover price. It's quite a bargain! Shipping and handling is just 50¢ per book in the U.S. and 75¢ per book in Canada.* I understand that accepting the 2 free books and gifts places me under no obligation to buy anything. I can always return a shipment and cancel at any time. Even if I never buy another book, the two free books and gifts are mine to keep forever.

105/305 IDN FEGR

Name _____ (PLEASE PRINT) _____

Address _____ Apt. # _____

City _____ State/Prov. _____ Zip/Postal Code _____

Signature (if under 18, a parent or guardian must sign) _____

LIREG11B

Love Inspired

Linda Goodnight

brings you a tale of a cowboy you can trust.

Rancher Austin Blackwell sees Annalisa Keller as a wounded person with too many secrets. This town is the perfect place for her to start over—just as it was for him. Trying to keep his own past hidden, Austin finds himself falling for Annalisa, whose warmth and love of life works its way into her heart…and promises never to leave.

Rancher's Refuge

WHISPER FALLS

Where every prayer is answered….

Available December 2012, wherever books are sold.

www.LoveInspiredBooks.com

LI87787